Stealth Magic 401
The Hellkitten Chronicles

By

Viola Grace

Imara wants nothing more than to find a different course, but stealth magic gives her the credits she needs to stay on track, and there aren't any other options rearing their heads.

Stealth Magic is not what she thought it would be, and the idea of breaking into a home to rob an ancient artifact for her final exam was a little daunting. Luckily, Imara has friends who are going to help her through training, some old and some new.

Through some work with the XIA, she finds a tutor for her training and a place to do it. Ritual Space offers her a welcome, and the inhabitants set themselves to the monumental task of her training. The exam is getting closer and time is a factor.

Mr. E just likes chasing the enchanted bunnies of Ritual Space.

Chapter One

oing push-ups in the living space with forty pounds of books on her back was not the way she wanted to be caught by Argus.

"You are supposed to read them."

She kept going through her set, and muttered through clenched teeth, "I know, but I got bored with that, so I am trying osmosis."

Argus crouched next to her, and she caught a very distinct lungful of the warm scent that made her cuddle with him at every opportunity. "You know that your kitten is on top of the books?"

She grunted and shoved upward again. "I suspected. I keep getting snickers in my brain, and I am definitely not laughing."

She finished her set and collapsed on the rug, sending tomes of magic and her kitten to the floor.

"So, how is the physical training going?"

She muttered against the wool fibres, "Fantastic. Give me five minutes, and I will be ready to head out with you."

He chuckled. "You look half dead."

"I will wake the other half, I promise." She pushed herself upright and gave him a quick kiss. Before he could make a grab for her, she jumped to her feet and headed up the stairs.

A magic wave scrubbed her skin clean while she peeled off her exercise clothing and yanked on her date-night outfit. Her domestic magic course had not gone to waste.

Jeans and a lace-up shirt were just the things, and as she headed back downstairs, her familiar jumped onto her shoulder with a determined bit of claw work.

You are not leaving without me.

She sighed. *Eventually, I am going to want to be alone with Argus.*

Not until you have graduated.

Spoilsport.

They are your rules; I am just making sure that you adhere to them.

She made a face and kept going as if she didn't have a fluffy chaperone on her shoulder. He was right, they were her rules. She had decided early on that no man was worth interrupting her education, but every now and then, when she and Argus were cuddled and watching a movie, she wanted to try to have it both ways.

"Okay, ready."

Argus smiled brightly, his appreciation glowing in his eyes. "This is going to be the best undercover operation I have ever been on."

She grinned and linked her arm with his. "Shall we? I have never been to a carnival before."

Mr. E wriggled with excitement. He was up for it as well.

"Never?" Argus's shock was apparent.

"Nope. How many times do I have to tell you that I have been sheltered by choice?" She waved at Reegar on their way out.

"I suppose it still seems peculiar to me. I apologize." His smile said he wasn't particularly contrite.

They walked to his SUV, and he tucked her inside. She buckled up, and Mr. E jumped onto the dashboard.

Argus got behind the wheel and buckled in. "He really loves to pretend he is driving."

"Yes. It is one of his favourite parts of modern life."

He started the vehicle and started the

long drive to the carnival outside Red-
bird City.

"Thank you for doing this, by the
way."

She smiled. "The XIA is compensat-
ing me for my time via the Death Keepers. My rise to Master is really paying
off."

He grinned as they went around the
on-ramp toward the city. "How did the
last mage guide tour go?"

Imara smiled and leaned back. "I am
getting the hang of it. The repositories
and memorial gardens are lining up to
get me in, and the mage guides are doing the same."

"Is that good?"

"It is very lucrative. It means that I
will be able to afford a decent set of fur-
niture when I open my office."

"You charge for taking the kids to the
repositories?"

She wrinkled her nose. "No, the mage

guides don't pay. The repositories pay the Death Keepers guild for my services and the rise in recruitment. There are teens taking the initial exams to determine aptitude for being Death Keepers because of the tours. Apparently, I make the tours *less creepy*."

He laughed.

"So, how are the guys? Are they upset that they aren't with us?"

"Oh, they are going to be there, but it would look a little odd if we all arrived in the same vehicle."

Imara nodded. "Makes sense, so shall I be all giddy or fawn all over you?"

"Just have fun. When you have fun, your face lights up, and everyone around you catches your joy."

She blushed so hard she felt like her shirt melted.

Mr. E was asleep on the dash, and his snoring distracted them both. He had a mature man's snort in a tiny kitten's body.

"Are Ivor and Lio going to be here?"

"Eventually. They will be arriving the moment that the sunset is firmly entrenched."

She smiled. "Right. Good. Sorry, but I am imagining them together on a carousel."

Argus chuckled. "No, not a carousel. They are far more inclined to ride a roller coaster."

"I am imagining Ivar eating a toffee apple."

Argus snorted, and they kept the conversation light while they drove the distance to the carnival. She paused and stared once. "Is that really Ritual Space?"

"It is. Adrea is a charming woman who will not suffer anyone to abuse her property. She runs the place with an iron grip, and it is refreshing to know that she will uphold the law."

Imara looked at the structure of the fencing that would keep any standard mage from climbing over it for a peek. "That is serious fencing."

"It is. Few folks are stupid enough to try and get in. The rabbits are always on guard."

She widened her eyes with delight. "Rabbits?"

"Bunnies. The story goes that folks brought them in for fertility rituals, but the bunnies escaped before they could be sacrificed. They fled through the grounds and have absorbed the magic of all the improperly executed spells."

"Wow. Do they have a leader?"

He chuckled. "They actually do. Aside from Adrea, they answer to a bunny named Blueberry."

"Wow. Good to know the chain of command if I ever need to go there."

"As you are in mage training, you probably will, at one point or another."

She grinned and looked back over her shoulder at the main entrance. "Maybe."

The rest of the ride was her holding his hand as they approached the carnival with its visible structures in the distance getting larger by the minute.

Mr. E tucked himself behind her hair as they got in line at the entrance.

She looked around her in amazement. Being raised in Sakenta City, she didn't have much experience with magical races, but time with Argus, Lio, and Ivor was helping considerably.

The smells of the carnival were amazing. Popcorn, sugar, deep-fried everything, and the chemical tang of toilets designed for crowds.

Argus paid for their entry tickets as well as a giant wad of ride tickets.

Imara linked her arm with his and nudged him with her hip. "So, where are we off to first?"

"Did you want to play some games? Go on some rides? Get a snack? I would recommend the last two in that order, by the way."

She chuckled. "I am expecting a proper meal after this."

"Of course. Now, do you want to try your hand at a ring toss, or maybe darts at a balloon?"

She wrinkled her nose and checked her pocket, pulling out a few bills. "I think that the hoop toss is about my speed."

"Hoop toss it is."

She smiled politely at the young man at the booth and said, "I would like to try, please."

He was bored, and he handed her three rings in exchange for two dollars. She glanced up at the wall of toys and then down at the pegs.

She looked at the ring, noted its imperfections, held it lightly, and threw it at the bottles in the centre of the booth. It sailed over the red-banded bottles and snagged on the black.

"Winner!"

She frowned. "What about my other two tosses?"

He raised his hands and stepped back. She focused again and struck the second and then the third black rings. Lights and sirens went off. The teen was screaming, "Winner!"

Imara blinked rapidly and looked at the barker. "What can I pick?"

He reached up and was going to give her the lion, but she held up her hand. "The black panther, please."

The youngster grabbed the medium-sized toy with fluffy fur and huge green eyes.

"Thank you." She smiled brightly and turned to Argus. Her date was bent over, laughing.

She linked her arm with his and

dragged him over to the darts. "I have something for Mr. E, now something for you."

It was another round of precision and checking the weighted darts, but she walked away with a lovely fluffy griffin for Argus, and he was still strangling himself with amusement.

"Those are fun. Now can we try a ride?"

He looked at his griffin and grinned. "Yes, of course. What do you want to do?"

She cocked her head up at the swings and wrinkled her nose. "I can already fly, so why not one of those ones that goes around backward?"

And so, they walked amongst the other folks out for a fun afternoon and drifted down toward the ride that let out a siren and then swirled backward on a loop.

She looked around and then she got

excited. "Can we go on that one instead?"

Argus looked down at her with his golden eyes resigned. "Are you sure?"

"Yes. Yes, I am."

And with her heroic and charming companion resigned, they got in line for the spinning teacups.

All Imara remembered of the ride was laughter flashed with a feeling of being rather ill.

She leaned against Argus and made a face. "That was a mistake."

"Yes, but it is one that you needed to make for yourself. Are you up for the haunted house?"

She looked at him with her eyes narrowed. "Does it mean we have to pass the food stall?"

"No. It is in the other direction."

"Excellent. Nothing like some fun and festive ghosts."

They got to the line, and she leaned

against Argus. He wrapped his arms around her and ran his hands up and down her spine like they were a normal couple.

When they were fourth from the front of the line, he lifted her chin on his knuckles. "Feeling better?"

"Yeah. Who knew that those little cups would make me and Mr. E so queasy?"

Her kitten was clinging to the side of the panther she had won, between it and her body. He was still looking a little woozy.

"They are famous for it, but you need to rack up these experiences for yourself."

She smiled. "Yeah, thanks for that. At least this one just goes around and tries to scare us."

"Yes, but a lot of couples use it as an excuse to make out."

"Is that a suggestion?" Her cheeks got

pink, she could feel it.

He smiled slyly. "Merely a commentary."

Imara could feel the pull of a spectre, but it was hard to pin it down. There was shielding in the way.

"I am going to feel so protected with you next to me, surrounded by all that metal."

He kept an arm around her and gave her shoulder a squeeze to let her know he was catching on.

The line moved forward, and the couple ahead of them got into the car. Imara watched the attendant lock them in with a snug-fitting bar, and she leaned her head against Argus. If he was snug, she should be able to get out if she needed to.

Their car came around, and she kept the stuffed animal and Mr. E between her and the bar.

Argus also slid his arm in between

them and flexed as the bar came down. The result was that as the car started moving, Imara had room to spare.

She cuddled up to Argus and smiled into the darkness, "Now, let's see what we can see."

The shadows flexed and twisted around them, and Imara looked around curiously. She had never been in a haunted house before. She looked forward to being frightened.

Chapter Two

Smara ignored the flopping synthetic mummies, the flashes of crimson light, and puffs of smoke-filled air. There was something in the ride that was adding to the creepy ambience, and she had only touched something similar once before.

Her senses went on the alert, looking for the accumulation stone.

When spectres began to lunge out at her, she knew she was close. Argus was flinching, but he didn't break character.

As a spectre of an old woman lunged at her, she screamed and burrowed close to Argus, curling her legs up and onto the seat. She pressed her familiar and the panther onto Argus's lap, and when they were under the mount for the stone, she lunged upward and captured it. The spectres ceased immediately, and she resumed her seat next to Argus.

"What was that?"

She whimpered. "Sorry I am so jumpy. The ghosts scared me."

Mr. E climbed into her lap, and she pulled the panther in to cover him as they went from dim light and loud noises to red sunset and thronging crowds.

The mechanism unlatched the restraint, and Argus left the car, taking her hand as he kept his griffin under his other arm.

He kept his arm around her as they walked down the steps. The attendant looked at her with a frown. "Is she okay?"

"It's her first carnival, and we started with the teacups. She's enjoying the novelty."

The attendant laughed; they headed back to the midway at a slow and steady pace.

Argus asked casually, "What did you catch?"

"A stone that shouldn't exist."

"Really? That is fascinating."

"Are they following us?"

"Oh, yes. We are going to make the exit before they catch up though, or we would if you fainted."

She smiled and stumbled. He picked her up and carried her through the exit, with folks murmuring in their wake.

Out in the lot, he kept walking toward his vehicle, but the multiple feet scraping on gravel proved that they had, indeed, been followed.

"Put the lady down and hand over the stone."

Argus turned with her in his arms, and he looked at the humans who were demanding the stone. "I am sorry. I don't know what you are referring to."

"Your lady friend grabbed a stone in the haunted house. We need it back. It is a vital component of our operation."

Imara looked them over and didn't see a Death Keeper in the bunch. She murmured to Argus, "They can't carry it."

"Why not?"

"Not Death Keepers. It isn't a soul stone; it is an accumulation of dying spectres. By themselves they are powerless, but together, they are a deadly force."

The leader of the men, a surly fellow, shouted, "Enough. Hand over the stone."

Imara kept her hand clenched, and she shook her head. "No. It's fucking dangerous."

Argus slid her to her feet, and Mr. E crept to her shoulder.

She stood with her hands at her sides. "I am not going to give up this stone. I don't want your deaths on my hands."

The guys blinked, and their spokesman said, "What the hell are you talking about?"

"You didn't put this in place. It was done for you by someone who specializes in death. This stone was getting stronger with each screaming client, and soon, the mages would have been strong enough to do more than gather stray energy, and the people they would feed off are those who are close to it at a fixed proximity."

The men looked at each other, and in the next heartbeat, full darkness fell. The XIA agents moved silently, and when the head of the thugs said, "Fuck it," and charged, the extranaturals moved in and took over.

Argus lunged forward, but he dropped his griffin. Imara bent to pick it up, and one of the thugs tackled her.

She went down to the gravel with a thud. Mr. E went flying.

A grubby hand scrabbled at her wrist, but she didn't open her hand. No one was getting that stone.

A low growl got the idiot's attention, and Imara's hellkitten had morphed into a hellcat once again. His eyes glowed with rich flames, and he grabbed the man clawing at her by the back of his shirt, flicking him away toward the parked cars.

He stood next to her while she got back to her feet. When she was standing and had the stuffies in her custody once again, she leaned on him and watched the zip-tying of the thugs from the haunted house.

Argus came up to her after glancing warily at Mr. E. "Are you all right?"

"Yes. I think so. I have a grip on the stone, and that is what matters."

"Imara, your hand is turning black."

She nodded. "I thought so. I am using my life force to wrap around the stone. It consumes me much more slowly than it does normal humans or other mages."

"Consumes?"

Mr. E's giant head lapped at her fist, and she opened it slightly. A moment later and her skin felt like skin again.

"What happened? Mr. E, what did you do?"

Her familiar looked at her with a smug demeanour, and he shrank back down into his normal fuzzy form.

Don't worry; I can regurgitate it when we get to a safe storage area.

Imara flexed her hand and ignored the kitten climbing her thigh, dangled from her shirt, and continued up her arm.

When he was settled against the back of her neck, she turned to Argus. "Well, he has it. So, now, we need a place to safely store it.”

“Can’t we take it to a repository?”

“No. This thing is dangerous. Degraded spectres are worn down to the basic compulsions. They want freedom, power, and life again. They can’t have the life, and it makes them angry, so they take what they can. They have no intellect; they can’t be reasoned with. They are formless ghouls. Creepy fuckers.”

He blinked. “Right. Well, where do you suggest?”

“A Death Keeper made this, so until we figure out who that was, it needs to be safe from interference.”

Lio came forward and offered, “Why don’t you contact Ritual Space? They might have some sort of facility for storing powerful artifacts.”

Argus pulled out his phone and dialled. “Good evening, Madam Adrea. My name is Agent Argus Dencroft with the XIA, and I need your help.”

Imara got a slight smile as Argus went into detail on the phone.

Why are you so happy?

He asked for help.

Her kitten snorted and rubbed his head against her neck.

Argus turned to her and extended his phone. "She wants to talk to you."

Imara took the phone. "Hello?"

"Hello, I am Adrea from Ritual Space. Who am I talking to and what do you have that needs our special brand of concealment?"

"My name is Imara Mirrin, I am a Master Death Keeper and a student at Depford College. The object that we need secure storage for is an accumulation stone. Some idiot Death Keeper has fused nearly a dozen faded spectres into one stone. This makes it an excellent power source for a weak mage, and it makes it a deadly weapon in the wrong hands. Until I can unravel and disperse the spectres, I need a safe place to put the stone."

"Can you do that?"

"Oh, yes. I have an affinity for the dead."

"How long will it take?"

"Well, provided that it goes smoothly, I should be able to disperse the mages in about eight weeks. I am a student, after all. It is a bit out of the way for me, but I can make it there once a week at your convenience."

"Have Argus bring you in. I look forward to seeing what you can do."

Imara smiled, though Adrea couldn't see her. "Thank you."

She hung up and smiled at Argus. "We are good."

"Really?"

"Yes, she will help us."

"How long can Mr. E hold that thing?"

"Two hours, tops. So, please, let's get

out of here."

Lio called out, "What do we charge them with?"

Imara answered, "Possession and use of an uncontained artifact of mass destruction."

Argus whistled and looked at Mr. E. "Right. Well, we had better get it somewhere safer. Get in the car, and I will get you to safety."

She nodded and looked out at the sea of dark SUVs. "Um. Give me a hint."

He walked up to one of the vehicles and opened the door. She hopped up and settled into the seat, buckling up and keeping her stuffed animals at her feet. Her live buddy she kept against her and kept a hand on as they left the carnival parking lot and headed back to the highway.

Her fuzzy buddy's body temperature was lowering. His normally warm little tummy was approaching her skin temperature.

Ritual space was less than half an hour away. They would have plenty of time.

"So, what was going on with your hand, precisely?"

She flexed her fingers. "It was dying slowly. It's an emergency response that I learned from Thomins. He was the one who offered me an apprenticeship, and he eventually pushed through my journeyman papers with the guild."

"A good man."

She snorted. "A man who liked to have someone to do the bulk of the maintenance on the spectre stones. He was a good friend, though, in as much of a friend as I had in those days."

Imara continued, "He taught me to block energy from my limbs in case of a thirsty spectre."

"Have you run into one of these before?"

She nodded. "Once. Death Keepers are given bonuses for clearing shattered and worn spectres from their memorial gardens or repositories. A friend of Thomins was filling in for a few hours while Thomins got some dental work finished up, and he took a stone out and showed it to me. I can only describe it as horrific. He had cleared out his fading section to make room for more spectres and stuffed the remaining traces of passed mages into the stone in his hand."

"Let me guess, Thomins came in."

"He did and beat the shit out of his friend. His friend dropped the stone, and I picked it up..." She trailed off, trapped in the memory.

"What happened?"

"The strongest of the spectres was leeching power from the weaker ones. They were all still there, the stronger roaring, the weaker screaming. The stronger one grabbed hold of me and tried to pull my energy out through the contact point. Thomins slapped it out of my hand, put it in a pouch, and called the authorities."

She rubbed her hand in memory. "When the guild officers were gone with Thomins' buddy, he started showing me how to defend myself against an accumulation stone."

"Does it always threaten your limbs?"

She looked at him and reached out to pat his hand. "Only when there are other targets that the stone could choose. Contact with me revs them up, and pulling in extranatural energy is very easy for them. It is why Death Keepers were created as a branch of the Mage Guild. We are needed if folks don't want embedded spectre stones to be draining life left and right out of all who pass."

"Deadly jewellery."

"Very."

He grabbed her hand and kissed the inside of her palm. "I am glad you made it out, fingers intact."

"Me too."

She kept tight to Mr. E, feeding him what she could via their connection. Her eyes scanned the horizon and watched for the first signs of Ritual Space. When the lights of the parking lot flickered in the distance, she nearly cried. Keeping her Death Keeper face on was the key to getting through this, but inside, she was sobbing with relief.

When she got out of the car, she stepped toward the gateway, just in time to watch it swing open.

"Imara? Welcome to Ritual Space. I am Adrea Morrigan, this is Officer Hyl Luning."

"This is Agent Argus Dencroft. Oh, and this is Mr. E, my familiar, and currently the fading containment of the stone."

Adrea smiled; her snow-white hair and bright blue eyes glowed in the limited light. "Come this way, and we will find you a gateway to safe storage."

Imara smiled gratefully. "Thank you. Mr. E, cough it up."

She set him on the white gravel, and she supported him while he went through the standard feline retching noises before the crystal fell. Imara grabbed it and scooped her familiar up. "Lead the way."

Adrea led them through the gateway, and Imara could feel the magic in everything around her. There was an outburst of life, and nothing could suppress it. "Wow."

Adrea smiled. "Thank you. It has been the work of generations to keep it this invigorated. I am sorry; I made an assumption. Is this your first time here?"

"Yes. No apologies necessary."

A white and blue flash appeared in

front of them. Adrea nodded and crouched to pet him. "This is Blueberry. He is effectively my butler. He will lead you to the position he deems safest for the stone."

"Don't you want..."

"No, I don't want to know where it is. Just follow the blue rabbit." Adrea winked. "I will put a kettle on."

Imara turned to Argus, gave him a thumbs-up and headed off in search of the bunny.

Chapter Three

Walking through the brush and into the shadows, she followed Blueberry until he led her to a gateway.

"Holy heck." She stepped through the wall between worlds and looked around at a pocket dimension filled with benches of stone and archways of energy.

The bunny hopped up on the bench and chattered at the arc.

Imara stepped forward and settled the stone into place. The energy in the archway grabbed it and held it in mid-air. The power had the signature of inert gel. The stone would get no purchase there. There was no power for it to consume.

Imara reached out and withdrew her power from the stone, filtering it through Mr. E until they were both back to normal strength.

Well done, Mage.

"Thank you. Now, I hope that bunny is willing to lead us back."

The blue and white escort waggled his puff of a tail and hopped out of the building, leading the way.

Imara followed the rabbit and waited for Mr. E to ask to be on his own four feet. He seemed content to ride along in her arms.

After the shadows and trees, they stepped out amongst berry bushes. A barely visible path led her to a backyard where Adrea was sitting with the two men, a tray of cookies, and a pot of tea. The entire area was illuminated by lanterns that were not attached to anything.

Argus got to his feet and came to her. "Imara, you have been gone for hours.

Are you all right?"

She blinked. "I thought it was just a few minutes."

Adrea winced. "Sorry. I forgot to regulate the temporal energy in that area. You lost a few hours."

She checked her watch, and it did, indeed, show that it was nearly midnight. "Damn."

Argus stayed next to her as she went to have a seat. Adrea poured her some tea, so Imara grabbed a cookie.

Adrea smiled and asked, "So, you are at Depford College?"

Imara swallowed her mouthful of chocolate chip cookie, and she mumbled, "I am in accelerated general studies."

Hyl smiled. "What does that entail?"

Argus grinned. "Taking a bunch of mindboggling courses to add skills that most mages can't manage."

Imara ignored his words but patted

his leg. "I am taking a number of high-credit courses to get a mage degree as quickly as I can so I can open my own spectral consulting agency."

Hyl nodded. "Nice. What is your next course?"

She glanced at Argus and then looked back to Hyl. "Stealth Magic."

Hyl looked shocked and amused. He pulled a card out of his pocket, wrote something on the back, and handed it to her. "When they ask you if you have a tutor, say yes."

Adrea looked between the two of them. "Is there something I should know?"

Argus was looking suspiciously at the business card. "Why does she need you?"

He informed the group of them. "Stealth Magic is a difficult course. On the first day, you are going to be offered a tutor. Once you have that tutor, you will need six to eight weeks of intensive training to work your body, your spells, and your nerve. On the last day of actual class, you will be given your assignment. It usually entails breaking and entering into the house of a prime family to re-trieve an easily identifiable heirloom. You bring it to your instructor, and you pass."

Imara's eyes bugged out. "Are stu-dents arrested?"

"All the time, but if they have their course assignment sheet with them, they are usually just dismissed, as long as they are caught on the date of the exam."

Imara ran her left hand through her hair. "Shit. It is too late to cancel the course."

Adrea lifted her hand. "If you have a secure space, I can link a temporary gateway to you. You can come and go for training. Hyl lives here, so he is here more often than not."

Hyl smiled. "Not many women pass the course. It would be my honour to help you through it."

Argus looked at the gathered folk. "I can help as well."

Imara looked to Hyl and took in the silence of his figure. He had training, and she guessed that some of his assignments ended in death.

"Argus, you are distracting as hell when you are around me. It is wonderful when we are together, but I can't imagine concentrating when you are next to me. Also, I can't work out at the college if I am understanding Hyl correctly. This is a very competitive course, right?"

He nodded. "I took it years ago, but I can't imagine that it has changed much."

Imara stroked Mr. E and looked around. "Thank you. I will take you up on that offer."

Adrea grinned and clapped her hands. "Excellent. When do you start?"

She bit her lip. "My course starts in thirty-nine hours."

Adrea nodded. "Good. I will lay in some extra supplies."

Hyl chuckled. "It isn't a tea party."

Can I go and play with the rabbits?

Imara looked down at a sheepish Mr. E. *Don't chase them. They are not food.*

I know. They glow with power. The damned kitten wants to play.

She set him down, and he went bounding over to the bunnies on the grass. There was a moment of introduction and then black tumbled around with white and grey.

Adrea blinked. "He is a very fun familiar."

"I know. He isn't fond of being a kitten unless he is standing in a banana cream pie. Perhaps coconut in a pinch."

"Is that good for him?"

"He isn't an actual cat, so yeah, it's fine. He gets a little gassy but is blissed out for days. The bunnies just looked like fun to the beast brain that comes with the fluffy body."

Hyl looked at her. "He won't be able to be with us while you train."

"That is fine, as long as he can run around and play here, he will be fine."

Adrea smiled. "While you are here for training, can you start on that stone? It is weighing the area down."

"Oh, sure. If I can get some pebbles from around here, I could even start taking it apart tonight."

Argus grumbled. "No. Not tonight. You have already changed colour in your extremities; no more spectre manipulation tonight."

Adrea got to her feet. "Right, speaking of pebbles, I will give you something to use to make a portal."

Imara sat in surprise. "Right. I will have to make a portal."

It isn't hard. I can show you the best

book.

She glanced at the critters and stifled a laugh as Mr. E rode the much larger Blueberry around the yard and through the gardens.

Argus was chuckling, and Adrea let out a snort when she returned. "That is something I am going to remember."

The way it was said, it was as if the space was going to remember it.

Adrea wrapped an arm around Hyl and leaned forward with her hand extended. "Here you go. Four stones from Ritual Space. Set them out in a box formation, step through a mirror, and you will be here in no time. Only a first level transport chant is needed. From here, I can boot you home."

"And when the training is done, I bring them back?"

Adrea grinned. "If you like. If we get along, you can keep them for visitation purposes."

Imara looked at the small black rocks. "What if someone steals them, tries to break in here?"

"Well, first, you are going to text me to let me know that you are coming. But the stones are also keyed to you and your familiar. No one else can get in on your ticket, so to speak."

Relief flowed through her. "Right. Yes, thank you. That is a relief."

A small paw clawing at her jeans got Imara's attention. Blueberry had a small drawstring bag in his teeth with R and S entwined on it. "Just in case I forget. Thank you, Blueberry. Did you throw Mr. E?"

She looked around, and the kitten in question was napping in a pile of bunnies. That was a lot of fluff.

"He is out for a few minutes. Have some tea. Recover from your evening." Adrea didn't look much older than Imara, but she seemed to have centuries of calm.

Her host poured the tea, and Imara held the delicate cup for a moment, inhaling the herbal scents that were soothing and invigorating at the same time. A first sip said that the tea had the same properties.

Imara drank the tea and felt a tingling down her left arm. The gravel abrasion from the fight was going from angry red to pink as she watched. "Okay. So, healing potion?"

Adrea sat and poured her tea from a different pot. "No, just herbs from Ritual Space. I, myself, can't use any magic. I am just a curator."

Hyl snorted. "Yes, she is a curator of everything you see around you. It all comes when she calls, one way or another."

Argus looked at Imara. "I know that feeling."

She smiled brightly at him. "I text. I

don't call."

The group laughed, and Imara finished her tea.

Imara sighed on the ride home. "Sorry that we had to take the detour, but I am delighted that I got a tutor out of it. I had no idea that this course would involve breaking and entering."

"Imara, promise me that you won't be involved in illegal activity."

"I promise. I am only going to engage in the exact requirements of my course."

"Will you quit the course?"

"No. There is nothing comparable for credits."

"Will you promise me you will be safe?"

She smiled. "Always. I have plans, you know."

He chuckled. "Yes, I know."

She stroked Mr. E and pulled tufts of white fluff from his midnight fur. It was a strangely serene drive home.

Reegar was waiting for her when she entered the hall. "Why were you out so long?"

"We found the problem and fixed it, but then, we needed to store it some-where safe, so we had to go there and time got away from me."

She grimaced at the babble, but it was all accurate.

The hum and click from the floor above indicated that Bara was still awake. "Is she still weaving?"

"She has taken to it. She has started looking into specialized fabrics, but the selection of options is very limited." Reegar pointed to the table nearest the library. "Sit, and I will get you some tea. I want to hear all about it."

She smiled. "Yes, of course. At least you won't balk if I have to do something illegal."

"The test for the stealth magic? Yes, I am aware of it. I have had a few incursions here to try and take my stone from the building. Those were in the days before you arrived, and so I had to resort to poltergeist methods and calling campus security."

"So, you won't mind if I study for the exam?"

He grinned. "You have had an interesting evening if someone outlined the exam for you. Start at the beginning."

She started at the beginning, and just as she reached the fight, Bara came down and pulled up a chair.

The mention of Ritual Space earned her a gasp, and when she detailed the requirements of the exam, Bara sat up with a jolt. "I have just the thing. I am working on an adaptive fabric, and it takes a day just to make a small strip, but I should have enough to cover you in a month."

"And Mr. E?"

She blinked and grinned. The kitten in question was passed out on a spell book. "Of course. Right, you would take him with you."

"Yeah, he won't train with me, but he will be with me on the day."

"Then, he shall have enough to wrap him as well. This is exciting."

Reegar grinned. "She isn't wrong. Can I do anything?"

"I need to find a level one transport spell. Just enough for me and Mr. E."

Reegar looked at her familiar and smirked. "Would you believe he is sleeping on the book?"

Bara snorted. "So, if it is competitive, what will you do to make them think you are training at the college?"

"Kitigan has been after me to jog with her. I am fairly sure that the schedule can be flexed to accommodate a run in the morning. If I have to go to the gym while they try and do me in, I will just have to go."

Bara nodded. "Right. I think I have a plan for that as well. This really is fun."

Imara shook her head. Four co-conspirators and she hadn't even started the course yet. It was the antithesis of stealth.

Chapter Four

"**I** am Professor McClairie, and this is Stealth Magic 401. You will learn how to be silent, invisible, and think on your feet, but to do that, you have to train." The professor paced in front of the scant dozen students in front of him.

He raised his hand and waved a sheet of paper. "In my hand, I have a list of the contact information of twelve volunteers who are willing to train you with a goal toward your final exam. They know what will be required."

Imara raised her hand, and he paused.

"Yes?"

"What is the format of the course?"

He gave her a pitying smile. "You will train, you will come back to get your exam information. You will fail, and you will probably cry."

A loud, braying laugh got her attention from across the small space. *Great, another brother.*

"Edgar Demiel, you have the first pick of names." The professor walked over to him and handed him the page. "When you have made your choice, strike it out. Once you have the information, you are dismissed until the next class date where you will get your assignment."

The professor went through the class in no particular order. What rapidly became apparent was that he was saving her for last.

The last student had scribbled on the page, and the professor passed it to her.

"The pickings are slim, but I am sure you will find something to suit you."

"We are allowed tutors from off this

list, correct?" She smiled brightly and got to her feet.

He blinked in surprise. "Yes, you are."

She extended the card that Hyl had given her. "He has volunteered to be my tutor."

He looked at the card and paled. "Why would he... how would you even meet him?"

"Oh, I had to do some work with the XIA last night, and we ended up at Ritual Space where he makes his home. He admired my attitude, and as he had already passed this course, he offered to train me for it."

The professor made a strangled sound. "What did you do with the XIA?"

"My job. They subcontracted me via the Death Keeper Guild. I was uniquely suited to the situation."

"Death Keeper?"

"Yes, don't you have files on your students?" She clued in, "Or do you only bother with the ones from prime families?" She tutted. "Do your homework, Professor. You missed something."

She took the business card back and nodded politely. "Good day, Professor."

She left the classroom with Mr. E chuckling madly on her shoulder.

Right, she was in it, and her friends were all on board. It was time to get busy with her portal work. Reegar had gotten clearance via the Chancellor's office for transports within the Hall, so she was clear, as soon as she could manage the transport. It was not a method of magic she had even considered. This was not going to be pleasant.

"Did she actually suggest a mirror portal?" Reegar was shocked.

"She did, but she also said she didn't do any magic."

He frowned and paged through the tomes. Mr. E jumped on the table with the small pouch in his teeth.

Imara smiled. "Oh, yeah. She gave me four stones from Ritual Space. Will that help?"

Reegar looked at the pouch as if it held pure gold. "Those are stones from the actual space?"

"Yes."

"Pure and not enchanted?"

"Yes."

He sat back and exhaled. "This is easy. You just need a measuring tape and a wall."

"I don't need a mirror?"

He waved that away. "It is considered to be necessary by the weak, but I find it tacky. It is more dangerous for the mage to use a mirror than just use energy to formulate a door. You are strong enough to do the job without the prop."

She blushed and was going to reply, but across the space, Bara's hand shot into the air. "I have a measuring tape.

Three, actually."

"You need to take her height, width at her widest point and the height of her average stride."

Mr. E jumped up and onto her shoulder, sitting with his head high.

Imara grinned and waited for Bara to come back and do the measuring. Her grin faded when she took a look at Bara's fingers. "What the hell is that?"

"Oh, blisters and splinters. The fibre I am working with isn't very friendly."

"Damn. I have a recipe for a healing cream."

She shook her head. "Cream makes my hands softer, and that makes the problem worse. I will toughen up."

While Imara stood there in shock, Bara quickly got her measurements, paused and cocked her head. "Can I use you as a model for my dressmaking class?"

With all Bara had done for her, Imara

nodded. "Of course."

"Excellent. I am looking into making a utility belt that is actually useful."

"A utility belt?"

"That fits with a formal gown." Bara smiled. "Here you go. Metric and imperial measurements. Don't mix them up." Bara gave her a fierce look and winked. "Arms out to your sides and hold still."

Ten minutes of precise—and occasionally tickling—measurements later and Imara was free to study the spell.

It was bizarrely easy. She just needed to place the stones out and power them up then speak the name of her destination. It would only work if someone were waiting for her on the other side.

"You should set up the stones on your wall using glue."

She nodded at Reegar. "I will tape them up until the glue holds."

"It isn't necessary. Go into the lab and find the super stick adhesive. It will bond in two seconds, so be quick."

She nodded, gathered the book and got the notes that Bara had left. Mr. E followed her into the lab, and he sat quietly on the counter until she found the adhesive.

What followed was a relatively easy procedure. Measure, mark, measure again with a different pen, and when she was sure, she took out the stones and brushed the adhesive on the back. She wore gloves and ended up having to cut one free when they were all in place. The adhesive was sealed to stop a comical moment, and she took it downstairs.

Are you ready?

"No. I am not ready, but the spell is easy. All I have to do is text her, and we can walk through."

Do it.

She took the number that Adrea had given her, and she entered in the new contact. She sent the first text. *Hi, it's*

Imara. Can I come through?

She waited for three minutes, and then, her phone chirped. *Come on over. Dress to sweat. You have one hour to use your portal.*

"Oh, shit. Right."

Imara quickly got an exercise bag together with bottles of water, put on a set of grubby sneakers, and when Mr. E was on her shoulder, she stood in front of the stones and powered them up the same way she offered energy to a spectre. A moment later, she was looking at Ritual Space, and Adrea was sitting and reading a book in her garden.

The scene was so idyllic, Imara hated to ruin it.

Imara stepped through, and after a short moment of disorientation, she settled on the other side with her familiar on her shoulder.

Adrea waved at her. "You made it!"

Imara nodded, and Mr. E was kneading her shoulder. "Yes, Mr. E, you can go play."

He was off her shoulder and bolting after some bunnies who waited for him before leading him into the undergrowth at high speed. Imara could hear him giggling via their connection.

"Hyl will be here within the hour, but he said I should start you on a few things."

There was a stack of books in the centre of the table, and each book had a bookmark hanging through it.

"Each of these has a spell necessary to what you are going to be doing, so he suggested you begin studying until he arrives. Once he does, you are heading to a special section of the space that I have put aside for your training."

Imara sat and pulled one of the books toward her. "I don't know how to thank you two."

"Pass your exam. Hyl says that women are frequently sabotaged in the course, so he wants you to shove it in McClairie's face."

"Ah. Well, that does explain the major dicks in the room." Imara smirked and opened the first book. The spell that he marked was *Surface tension and wall climbing*. It was a good place to start.

By the time Hyl had arrived, she had made it through *Obscuring the scent of magic,* and *Passing through*. She was in the middle of *Pulling shadows* when Hyl walked in and gave Adrea a kiss that turned her bright red.

Hyl lifted his head and smiled at Imara. "Are you ready to work?"

"I am."

"Good. There is a pack under the table, bring the books."

She scrambled to put the books in the pack, and she shifted it to her back, grabbing a bottle of water.

"Where is your familiar?"

"He is off playing with the bunnies."

"Good. It is better that he is occupied. This is going to take a while." Hyl nodded, turned, and jogged off toward the nearest stand of trees.

Imara turned back and smiled at Adrea. "See you later!"

Adrea waved her on.

Imara turned her back on her host and ran after her tutor.

Hyl was walking briskly, but no matter how fast Imara ran, she could never quite catch up with him.

The books were excessively heavy, but she just hitched the straps tighter until they moved with every step she took.

She chased him for half an hour before she burst out of the forest path and ended up in an open field with a wide tower in the centre of it. Hyl was standing near the bricked tower.

She ran up to him and paused. "What

next?"

"Climb it."

She looked up at the tower and back to him. "Pardon me?"

"I have observed your musculature, you will be able to support yourself, so you have two hours to climb the tower and then, I will help you with your technique."

She stared at him. "You are kidding."

"I am not. You can use any method that you can to get to the second story."

She paused and nodded. "Including the books on my back."

"Correct. I am here if you have questions, but figuring things out for yourself is more useful. We can tweak the technique from there."

It was a challenge she wasn't backing down from. She got the pack settled firmly on her back and stepped forward.

Chapter Five

Smara fell on her ass three times before she used the sticking spell. Once she had placed the spell on her body, she was able to press her body against the wall and use it as a point of grip as she slowly crept upward.

"Well done. You read the books?"

"A few of them." She grunted and pushed up with her foot while reaching with the opposite hand. "The ones that were bookmarked."

"Bookmarked? Huh." Hyl chuckled.

She reached up, and her hand hit open air. She glanced up and exhaled.

"Now for the hard part. Come down slowly. Be sure of your footing."

She didn't nod, she just did as he suggested. Her hands were aching, her toes were cramping, but she still moved down, row by row.

When she hit solid ground, she dropped like a stone. She sat on the ground, her knees splayed, feet curled inside her shoes, and her fingers wrapped inward to stop their raw throbbing.

Hyl looked her over and nodded. "I will be right back."

He went into the tower and emerged a minute later with a thermos flask. He crouched next to her and poured a cup. One look at her hands and he held the cup to her lips. "Drink it. It is the same tea that she gave you the other day but with nettles to help make your skin more durable."

She swallowed and winced at the burn of the tea. The last time it had been cool.

He pulled the cup back. "It has to burn to toughen your skin. How are your hands?"

She flexed them, and the raw and bloody fingertips were healing over. "Are you sure she doesn't use magic?"

He chuckled. "No. The herbs are grown here, and they have their own magic."

"Do they work outside the space?"

"Sure. Adrea is just getting her online shop ready. The sales will be by invitation only after the purchaser has passed a security check, but yeah, she is going digital."

"Nice. She will sell out in seconds."

Hyl chuckled. "I am not so sure. Most mages have some kind of legal trouble in their histories. If they do, we will find it."

"So, getting caught during my exam would knock me off the list."

"No, but getting caught the day after

would."

She pulled her legs up and rested her forearms on her knees. "So, I have one night to finish the exam?"

He grinned. "That is where folks get it wrong. You have twenty-three hours and fifty-nine minutes."

Imara stared at him. "So any time during that day. Oh, wow. That makes things easier and exponentially harder."

"How harder?"

"I don't know what the best time would be. This is going to take some research."

"You will figure it out. That is one point where I can't advise you. All I can do is give you the physical skills to engage in your stealth manoeuvres."

"Right."

He nodded. "Now, do your hands feel better?"

She looked at them and nodded. "They do."

"Good. Now get back up the tower and try to keep it under two hours this time."

She widened her eyes. "It took longer than two hours?"

"Yes, it did. Now, get up and get down in under two hours."

She nodded and grunted as she got to her feet. She faced the tower, summoned the sticking spell, and crawled upward as quickly as she could. This time, her limbs obeyed her, and she was able to move along the stone in what felt like a few minutes.

The moment she got down to the base, she turned to him. "How long?"

"One hour and twenty-two minutes. Very good for a first day."

She groaned. "It felt so fast."

"It will. The thing you have to remember is that you can't depend on your perception of time. You have to move as rapidly as possible to throw off the effects of the spells you will need."

"The sticking spell. It makes me slow."

He grinned. "It does. It keeps you on the wall, but it takes four times your normal speed."

She exhaled and then looked at him. "What else for today?"

"You want to do more?"

"I do."

He nodded. "Right. Back up the tower. When you can get to the top and back down again in five minutes, we can work on the next task."

She looked at the tower and the small smears of blood she had left behind. With a focus on increasing her speed, she muttered the spell, jumped to stick herself to the wall and hauled herself as fast as she could. When she was down, he applauded slowly. "Excellent, but still twenty minutes."

She whirled and climbed the wall for

the fourth time, this time without the sticking spell.

She slipped a few times, but it made her faster. She climbed up twenty feet and then lowered herself back down again with careful dexterity.

Hyl grinned and applauded. "Excellent. This time, you are dead on five minutes. Now, let's go and get some food. Adrea is waiting."

Her limbs told her that she had been climbing for days, but Mr. E's perky face when they made it back to the gardens told her that it had barely been any time at all.

He ran up to her and waited until she had shucked the pack off her shoulders before he jumped up and rubbed against her sweaty face with his fuzzy one.

I had a marvellous time. When do we come back?

She looked to Hyl. "When is our second class?"

"Tomorrow will be too soon, but Thursday should be fine."

She scowled. "I don't want to interfere with your work."

Adrea waved that off. "He is assigned as my bodyguard, and he only leaves when I authorize it. I am willing to hang onto him as long as you need him."

Hyl grinned and handed Imara a platter full of sandwiches. "Eat. You need it."

She dropped into her chair with a thud.

Adrea gave her a commiserating look. "Hard, huh?"

"Yeah. Thanks for that tea. I was wondering if I could buy some when you get up and running. A friend is helping me, but the material she is working with is tearing up her skin something awful. I think that tea would be just the thing."

Adrea got to her feet and walked into the house.

Imara blinked at Hyl. "Did I say

something wrong?"

"No, just wait."

Adrea came out with a large muslin bag. "Here. I have divided it into doses. Have her drink one when you see her and then another one twelve hours later. You need to do the same, or tomorrow, you won't be able to move."

Imara was eating as if had been days and not hours since she last had a meal.

She cleared her mouth. "Day after tomorrow. Same time as today."

Hyl grinned. "Deal. Just so you can prepare yourself, the tower is getting higher."

She smiled and nodded. "I figured. Well, at least I can practice the spell and work on my technique at the hall."

A half-hour of polite chitchat later, Adrea sent her home.

"Now that I know where your portal is, you can come through anytime. I am opening it so you can get a clear run home."

She confirmed with Hyl, "I leave the books?"

"You leave the books. These are for Ritual Space use only."

She nodded, grabbed the bag she hadn't used, and ran for the open portal with her familiar on her shoulder. She stumbled into her bedroom. Shower. The shower was her first port of call.

Once she was no longer covered with blood and sweat, she grabbed the muslin bag and took it down to Bara. Without asking her, she made a pot of tea and poured her a cup. "Drink this."

Bara leaned back, suspicious. "Why?"

"Because it will heal you and help toughen your hands without losing dexterity. It is a gift from the owner of Ritual Space."

That was all it took. Bara finished the whole pot, and she sat there shivering and flushing as the effects were all seen in her body. The moment her hands cleared up, she sighed in relief.

"What is that stuff?"

Imara settled at the table. "Herbs from Ritual Space. It's a gift from the owner."

Bara looked at her cup as if she wanted to bronze it. "Have you been there?"

"Yeah, it is where I am training. That is what the portal was for."

Bara looked at her with a wistful look. "When you are done training, can I come, too?"

"I will ask. I think it will be fine."

Bara grinned. "That is definitely something to look forward to."

Imara nodded, gathered the rest of the herb packs, and handed one to Bara. "Drink this in twelve hours. According to Adrea, that should do it."

"I feel so much better; I don't know what another dose could do."

"She's an herbalist, so if she says to

drink it, drink it.”

Bara took her phone and set the alarm. “There, that should bring me out of my weaving stupor.”

Imara chuckled.

“So, what are you doing tonight?”

“I am applying to the Death Keeper Guild for a dozen empty soul stones. I need to keep a promise to Adrea about dealing with the rock I found the other day.”

Bara nodded. “Right, well, I feel so much better, I am heading back to the loom.”

“Enjoy. Don’t forget your phone.”

“Yes, Ma’am.”

Imara sighed and looked around. There was no sign of Reegar, which was odd. He was always around.

She reached out with magic and located him. Blushing furiously, she withdrew. Liirick was in town, and they were engaged in a private moment.

Mr. E hopped up onto the table and stretched. *I could have told you that.*

She scratched his chin. "Did you have fun with the bunnies?"

We told jokes for the first six hours, and then, they brought me to Adrea for a snack. She kept me busy for an hour, and then, we went to play again.

She frowned. "What? We weren't there that long."

Well, I am a cat, my observation of the time period could have been skewed.

I hope so. She checked the time and date on her phone and sighed in relief. She was right where and when she was supposed to be, but she didn't put it past Ritual Space to knock time around... again.

With nothing do to and no one to talk to, she sent the email to the Death Keepers, and then, she went to look for spells that might be useful while she was breaking into a magical building full of people. Some kind of bladder control might be in order.

Hyl was peeling an apple with a knife. "Do the warm-up."

She nodded and scaled the six stories of smooth brick, and then, she worked her way back down. They were in week three of her six weeks of training, and this was now an experience she was used to.

When she was standing at the base of the tower again, she caught her breath. "Now what?"

He smiled. "Inside the building, I have hidden a valuable object. Once you retrieve it, you will have to find your way out of the building again. It will not be easy. Go."

She nodded and used the door-opening spell that she had already practiced. So far, he had left her chocolate, a glass of water, and a happy kitten on a post-it note.

Imara moved through the rooms as quickly as she could until she found the valuable object. She scooped Mr. E up from the basket where he had been sleeping, and she turned to the doorway she had entered by. The wall sealed, and there was no trace of a doorway.

She winced. She had been afraid that this was that spell. She held the still-sleeping Mr. E tight to her chest, and she cast the *pass-through* spell. She stepped through the one wall, and all other walls were solid again.

She turned and looked around her, orienting herself to the tower she was in. She approached her chosen wall and passed through it, waiting until she was on the other side before she gasped. The air was fresh, and the green grass stroked her ankles.

Hyl applauded as he approached her. "Well done. The shortest distance was through the outer wall. The only problem lies in if you are on an upper floor, so that is where we will practice next."

Mr. E disappeared from her arms, and she ran around to the point where she could sense him, and she climbed the wall before entering via the window. She grabbed him and was planning to go back out the window, but it had paved itself over.

His sleep wasn't normal, so she made an executive decision. She stepped to the wall, placed them within it and used the molecular resistance to drop them to the main floor. When she felt solid ground beneath her feet, she forged forward along the line of the wall until she was outside.

Hyl nodded. "Right. Enough of that for today. Time for lunch."

She smiled and breathed deeply. "In a moment. Emotion and spell casting don't mix."

Mr. E started to squirm in her arms, and Hyl nodded. "Right. Sorry, but it was necessary to see how you would do with a living being."

She nodded. "I understand. It is also why I have the weight on my back the whole time."

He shook his head. "You will see what a difference that makes when you are done with your training. If it makes you feel better, there are only two exercises left, and they can both be combined. Drawing shadows and hiding traces of your presence. After what you have been doing, they are mainly mental exercises. Once those are mastered, you can continue to come here to practice, but you won't need me anymore."

"Can I practice now? It is only two weeks to my exam."

"Well, you are filthy, sweaty, exhausted, and reeking of magic. If you can walk back to the garden without being besieged by bunnies, I will consider you graduated."

Imara looked at the sleepy kitten in her arms, and she nodded. "You are on."

Chapter Six

Running the two spells together was difficult, and it meant she had to move slowly through the woods, careful to measure her steps. She might be in shadow with no scent of man or magic, but her footsteps still made noise.

Hyl was sitting with Adrea in the middle of a pool of light. Imara whispered for help to the space, and the lanterns dimmed. She stepped to the side and approached the chair she normally sat in, facing the herb gardens and the rioting rabbits. The moment she touched the chair, the spells dissipated.

Adrea laughed at Hyl's expression. "Hooray! You spooked him. How did you get the lamps to dim enough to give you cover?"

"I asked. You have told me enough about Ritual Space over the last few weeks to know that as long as what I wanted wouldn't affect you, it might just help me."

Hyl poured her a cup of tea. "I consider you a very successful student. Well done, Imara."

Adrea raised her cup. "Well done, Imara."

She blushed and looked down at her grubby hands. "Thanks. I still need to practice."

"And I am glad of the company."

Hyl chortled. "I am sure that Argus will be happy if you can spend a few more days with him."

Imara waved her hand through the air. "He knows what I am focused on. While he is right for me, I might not be right for him. If he changes his inclination, I won't hold it against him."

Adrea quirked her lips. "That is why you have kept it to a friendship."

"Until I can afford for it to be more, yes."

Hyl whistled. "You really do have a plan."

"Yes, and I am very lucky to meet the right people at the right time." She cupped her teacup in her hands, and she sipped slowly. For once, she wasn't served from a separate pot.

Adrea looked at Hyl, and her expression softened. "To meeting the right people at the right time."

They all toasted with their teacups over the table. Mr. E snorted into consciousness and stretched.

The talked softly of friends and families and how it was a great thing that you could at least choose one.

She scratched under Mr. E's chin as

they entered her room. She glanced back at the portal a moment before it closed. "I am guessing I won't have it much longer."

I would not be so sure about that.

"Technically, it would be dangerous for them to leave those stones with me."

True, but it is Adrea's choice. Her space, her choices.

She put him on the bed and grabbed her clothing for after her shower. "How do you think I did?"

I think that I only learned of your actions through your mind. You did very well. Hyl is a good teacher. He got the physical into your muscle memory and then moved on to the strategy.

"I know. I got lucky."

His chuckle was in her mind while she headed for her shower.

Kitty was waiting in the common room when Imara came down. "Ready for coffee and gossip?"

Imara checked her watch and blinked in surprise. The sky was still light, though she felt like she had been at Ritual Space most of the day. "Of course. Sorry. I lost track of time."

"You look exhausted. Even Mr. E looks sleepy."

"I will get some coffee and be right as rain. Are we walking?"

"Yes. It's a wonderful night."

"Great." Imara smiled. "I need some fresh, normal air."

"I can't guarantee normal, but it is definitely fresh. Get a coat."

Imara patted herself down to make sure she had her wallet, beckoned to her familiar, and then slipped on a loose poncho. Mr. E popped his head out the neck hole, and he got comfy.

"Okay, ready."

Kitty smiled and linked arms with her, hauling her out of the hall and down the street.

The restaurant was busy, but ordering quickly meant that they had time to chat while they waited for their food. Mr. E had his usual fans, so he sat at the edge of the table and let people stroke his chin.

"Okay, Imara, what have you been up to?"

Imara shrugged. "Working out, getting ready for the class exam. How about you?"

"My apiary is twelve feet tall, and I don't have the nerve to harvest the honey for testing." Kitty looked abashed.

Imara looked at her. "Do you need help? We could do it tonight."

Kitty looked at her with adoration. "Really? That would be wonderful."

"Sure. Let's just fortify ourselves first and then get the boxes for the frames and a ladder. We will get the honey out of the hive tonight... before they know what has happened."

Kitty sighed. "I have missed hanging out with you."

"Yeah, I am getting that a lot, but this course load is heavy. It is one class, but it takes all my time."

"I know. It just sucks. I only found you a few months ago. It is just that I want to hang out more."

Imara nodded. "I feel the same. So, tonight, we will make up for lost time."

"You still look exhausted."

"I can sleep in tomorrow." She toasted Kitty with a cup of coffee and took a swig of the hot brew. Their night was set.

Kitty spent the rest of the dinner explaining the technique for harvesting the honey with minimal interference with the bees.

They paid for dinner and Mr. E's dessert and headed over to the agricultural centre.

It felt just like the days that Imara had spent with the Deegle family. With the equipment and protective gear, they crept out to the apiary, and Kitty had not been kidding. The stack of boxes was actually twelve feet high, so Imara made sure that she had a box to catch the first rounds of frames with honey.

Imara was going to remove the frames and lower them one by one to Kitigan's gloved hands.

Imara removed the lid of the hive and pried off the inner cover. There were next to no bees near her as they were down keeping the brood warm, or so Kitty had promised.

She pried up the edges of the box and lifted it. The weight wasn't bad at all, considering her recent training, so she tucked it on one hip and moved down the ladder.

Kitty was staring. "How can you lift it so easily?"

"I told you, I have been working out."

She went back up the ladder and took down the next box the same way, shaking out a few bees and going down the ladder again.

The next level was the final one that she needed the ladder for, and the trolley that Kitty had grabbed took the hive boxes easily.

"How many more until I get to the excluder?"

"Just two."

Each level had more bees on it, but she shook off the slightly more agitated inhabitants and kept working her way down to the excluder.

The stack of brood boxes was chest high when she finished robbing them. Several bees were cruising around, but they didn't move far from the original hive.

Kitty handed her the empties, and Imara set them in place, evening out the frame spacing before putting the next on top. The cover and lid went in place, making the entire tower nine feet tall and ridiculous.

Imara descended the ladder and shook her head. "You are going to have to do this yourself, you know."

"I know. I am just afraid of getting stung. These little bastards pack a punch."

"Please, they are ladies." Imara laughed and carried the ladder to the equipment shed.

Kitty trundled the boxes into the lab, and Imara followed when the single-use gear was stowed.

In the lab, they prepped the equipment, removed their protective gear and began harvesting two hundred sixty pounds of honey with magical properties.

"What are you going to do with all this?" Imara stared at the settling vat that contained it all.

"Study it, try different enchantments, that sort of thing."

Imara didn't want to ask, but something made her. "Can I have a litre of it?"

"Sure. Let me get you a jar. What do you want it for?"

Imara rubbed her forehead. "I don't know yet. I just feel that I need it."

"Good enough."

The jar of honey was produced; Kitty made her notes on her records' chart, and Imara started yawning.

Kitty looked around and saw the clock. "Good lord, I have kept you all night."

Mr. E was snoring softly against her neck. Nothing woke him.

"It's fine. It was fun. What are you going to do with the extra bees?"

"They are nearing the end of their life cycle. Why? Do you have an idea?"

"I will make a call, and if you need a

place for them to go and sniff flowers all the year-round. I know just the spot."

Kitty smiled. "I will think it over."

"Good. I am going to head back to Reegar Hall. It has been a very long day."

"Thanks for coming out, Imara. I appreciate it."

Imara was turning to leave when she had a thought. "If you know anyone who is giving away a bike, let me know. I think it is another thing that will come in handy."

"Will do, now shoo!" Kitty grinned and waved her off.

Imara nodded and headed out the door. There were only a few security vehicles on campus, and her calm and even stride didn't raise their suspicions.

It took her twenty-five minutes to get to the hall, and she peeled off her wrap with a sigh, stumbling through the hall and up the steps until she got to her room. Changing her clothing was going to take too much effort, so she just dropped onto her bed.

Bara rubbed her shoulder. "Imara, come on. I have my exam in two hours, and I need to make final adjustments on the gown.

Imara sat up, and she flung her arms wide.

"Damn. Okay. Come with me, and I will do what I have to so you can get back to bed. Are you still ready to be my model?"

Imara nodded.

"Good. Now stay there, I will get the gown."

Imara was on autopilot as she was stripped, stuffed into eveningwear, and pinned.

"Wow, you have been working out. Impressive. This is going to look fantastic."

Imara nodded, and when the gown was gone, she thudded back into bed.

Imara woke fully in a strange environment with Bara fussing with her hair. Bara grinned. "There you are. Mr. E was willing to drive you on autopilot all day, but he was gravitating to ordering his own pizza, so I was hoping you would come to."

"I am so sorry."

"You have been burning the candle at both ends. I get it. Now, we are up next, walk with your head high with an expression that everyone is beneath you but amuses you."

Imara smirked. "That is my normal expression."

"I know. Down the runway, turn, and back up. No drama."

"Nothing dramatic. Got it." And so, barely awake, she walked up the steps, waited for the announcement of Bara's name, and she walked down the runway, wondering why the hell they had made it so long. At the end, she caught a look at what had to be her father, but this was a drama-free zone, so she kept walking back to the rear of the stage.

Bara's hug nearly crushed bones.

They waited backstage until the scores were announced, and when Bara was declared, "Ninety-eight," Imara was hauled onto the stage once again.

There was applause, she took a bow, and she had to wait for Bara's return after her fellow students applauded her because Imara had no idea where she was.

Mr. E rubbed against her ankles, so Imara reached down and picked him up. The population around her made cooing noises, and since he had driven her there, she offered him up for caresses and cuddles.

The party that Bara had planned was

extensive, but Imara only had to be there for the first twenty minutes. She scampered upstairs and checked the calendar. She hadn't missed it. Tomorrow, she would get her exam assignment and the rest of the time would be used for preparing her assault on whatever hall she was assigned.

Imara looked at the engraved document, and she looked back up at Professor McClairie. "You are joking."

"I am not. That is your assignment." He raised his voice. "Guard your assignments well, as your fellow students can find you, foil you, and use their skills to work against you."

Edgar Demiel was still sneering at her, and Imara had no idea why. She had his ancestral home on her card. *Demiel Hall,* on the twenty-seventh. It was the last place she wanted to be.

When the professor finished reading

out the rules of their exam, she stood up. Another card dropped in front of her, and when she looked up, Edgar was out the door.

She didn't look at the card until she was home, and Mr. E was fighting to cackle. It was hard with a kitten's face.

"What the hell?"

Reegar stepped over to her and looked over her shoulder. "You have been invited to a birthday party."

"It is my father's birthday party and an introduction to my first niece. This is... something is... damn it is the same day as the exam."

She huffed and sat down for a moment before Hyl's advice ran through her head. "It has to be that day but not during the day."

Bara looked up from where she was sewing together the wraps that would keep Imara from being glaringly visible during her adventure. "What does that mean?"

"That means that I am going to be doing a lot of night work, but this is all going to work out in the end."

Reegar grinned, Bara gave her a thumbs-up, and Mr. E stretched before going back to sleep on his favourite book. Now that the Death Keepers had taken off with the spectres from the accumulation stone, everything was finally coming together.

She might be able to master stealth magic with just a little help from her friends.

Chapter Seven

Smara had given up on telling herself that she was an idiot. She already knew it. Mr. E was wrapped in the same fabric that she was, and it appeared that Bara's weaving work was paying off. They were nearly invisible.

Demiel Hall was exactly where the map had shown her it would be. The magical sensors were at the edges of the property, and it was with a slow and casual motion that she walked past them, waiting for the alarm.

Hyl had been confident. She just had to act like she belonged there, and the grounds would accept her.

She moved calmly to the house and

used her fingers and toes in the brick and stone to pull herself upward. Mr. E was sensibly using her for transport.

When they made it to the second floor, she closed her eyes and looked for what she knew had to be there. A spectre stuck its head out and spoke.

"Should I alert the family?"

The words were faint, and Imara gripped the wall with her left hand and extended her right. The spectre ran her hand through Imara's and smiled. "A daughter of the Demiels? Well, well, what do you want here?"

Imara whispered, "The crystal. Just for three hours."

"Well, your timing is impeccable. They have been preparing to put traps in the chamber, but they won't put them in place until the morning."

Imara nodded and spoke low, "Can you open the window?"

"I can turn off the whole security system, but why should I?"

"I can give you enough power to let you take physical form when you want for a year."

Her ancestor grinned. "Deal. Do you want me to bring you the crystal?"

"Can you?"

"I can, I will give it to you now, child, and put it back when you bring it. Your soul does not shine with greed."

The ancestor disappeared for a moment. Imara hung on and felt the panic begin to take hold. The window opened, and the crystal fell the few feet into Imara's hand. She slipped a little of her energy into the crystal and felt the response.

She wrinkled her nose, and she waited. The slight ripple of shadow gave her what she needed, and when the weight returned to her shoulder, she took the crystal and headed down to the ground.

The bicycle was where she had hidden

it, tucked in the shadows.

Now, it was time for the most dangerous part of the evening. She rode over to Professor McClairie's home and cast an assessment spell. The professor was asleep in the study, main floor, rear.

She went to the back of the building and sent Mr. E a signal.

She stepped back against the building as her kitten gave a strangled yowl. The professor came out warily and looked around. With their wraps still on, they looked like bent landscape. If they didn't move, they were unseeable.

"Professor McClairie? I have completed my exam."

The face turned toward her with shock and his fist raised. "Who is it?"

She carefully parted her mask. "Mirrin, sir. I have my assignment, and I wish to register completion of my project."

"Show me the assignment."

She reached into the wraps and found the page that she had guarded with her life. "Here."

"The Lieth crystal, at Demiel Hall. Where is it?"

She extended the crystal to him, and the moment he touched the glowing blue crystal, it dulled.

"Well, Mirrin, this is a fail. This isn't the crystal."

Mr. E started hacking up a hairball, and the genuine crystal slid out of his throat and onto the grass.

Imara reached down and picked up the crystal, wiping it off on the grass before handing it over.

"Is it still wet?"

"No, he isn't really physical, so that sound was just for fun."

Mr. E was busy putting his mask back in place, and he soon disappeared.

The professor examined it, and he nodded. "You have done it."

A flash went off, and he blinked. "What was that?"

"A record that I finished in case you wake up thinking this is a dream."

"Oh, right. Why are you here now?"

"Ah, I wanted to return the crystal to the hall before anyone notices it is gone. Since they are so eager to set me up, I thought that I shouldn't let them panic. Plus, I have to go to a party there tonight, and all eyes will be on me. Breaking in before dawn to complete the assignment will be difficult, but if I leave now, I can manage it."

He grinned and handed her the crystal. "I normally just return it via a spell, but I like your idea. If you survive to attend class tomorrow, let me know how the party was."

She mentally cursed as much as she could manage, but she took the original and the dummy crystal, nodded her head, and Mr. E hopped on for a ride.

So, we could have just handed it over?

Yes. She got back on her bike and pedalled as fast as she could as the night crept on toward dawn.

I think I am going to do a pass-through.

Are you in a good state of mind?

Yes. Can you show me where to go?

So, you will carry me?

Of course.

This is getting exciting.

I have been learning, may as well use it.

She pulled up and tucked her vehicle deep into the bushes where she had set it before and saw the security vehicle pa-trolling the area.

Her heart pounded heavily, but when it continued past her hiding spot, she noted that it was a simple set of human mages behind the wheel.

Bara said this clothing could take a

shift. He looked at her.

I am trusting that she was right. Did you want to eat the crystals again?

Sure. It will be easier for you to get us through, and I will deposit them back in the chest. Side by side.

She set down the crystals and shielded them with her body while he swallowed them.

She exhaled and nodded in personal determination. *Let's go.*

Imara held still and felt her body melt and twist. When her contortions ceased, she flexed her wings and gave a few practice flaps. She was ready to fly.

I will snag you in the open.

I will try not to run.

She took a few steps and pushed down with magic as her wings propelled her upward.

A few heavy beats and she was high enough to get into open space. She climbed to about sixty feet, wheeled, and went looking for her familiar.

She found him by scent, not by sight. Imara dove down and grabbed him carefully, keeping her claws wide to snag him before she carried him up and over the peak of the hall.

Down to the third chimney. The northeast space.

Got it. Going pass-through.

Ready when you are.

Her wings thrashed the air as she cast the spell, and when she felt it working, she dropped through the roof using her flying magic to keep her from moving too quickly.

The layers of the building were exposed to her, but having trained for this, she was ready for it.

Next chamber down.

Got it.

She came through into a huge horde of magical artifacts. She dropped her kitten and hovered in the space, not touching down. The pass-through spell only worked on objects that she touched, but since her kitten was part of her body, she could scoop him up and carry him away later.

Mr. E moved like a professional. He climbed over a few displays until he reached a box that was open and tempting.

He did his hairball hack silently and brought up the genuine stone. Next to it, he brought out the fake. Just to let them know that their subterfuge had been discovered.

He finished with the deposit, and he pushed the lid closed with his little paws.

Imara kept herself in place, and when he jumped for her, she caught him, carrying him right out through the wall and into the night.

The security officers were near her bike, so she turned toward home and flew steadily.

The night was beautiful, and the dawn was pinking the edges of the sky. The stars mixed in with the lightening sky were gorgeous.

When she saw Reegar Hall, she headed to the familiar rooftop. The XIA vehicle down in the lot did make her nervous, but she wasn't doing anything wrong. Well, not *now* anyway.

She dropped Mr. E off, banked, wheeled, and landed on her own, down on one knee. She stood and pulled the wrappings from her face and hands. Mr. E was tucked up under her arm, and she headed to her room.

She heard voices downstairs but ignored them in favour of getting to her room and stripping off the wrappings, getting a normal outfit of underwear, jeans and a sweatshirt in place, just as Reegar knocked on the door.

"Imara, there are XIA agents downstairs."

She paused. "Argus?"

"No. Not Argus."

"What do they want?" She pulled her sneakers on.

"A Death Keeper."

"Oh. That I can help with. Be right down."

Mr. E finished his disrobing, and he hopped on her shoulder. *Not without me.*

"Right. Not without you."

She finished getting dressed, combed her hair, and flipped it over her shoulder, catching Mr. E in the face.

He dug his little claws into her skin, and she left her room to head downstairs.

The agents were not ones she had met before, but she had seen them that night at the carnival.

"Hello."

"Death Keeper Imara Mirrin?" The elf

was polite, but there was tension around his eyes and lips.

She inclined her head. "Yes, yes, I am."

"I am Iofer, this is Morgig and Henry. We have been sent to ask you to assist us in a matter involving a spectre."

She scowled. "I thought that was the Mage Guild's issue."

"That is the problem. Please, come with us."

If he didn't have panic in his eyes, she would have turned to Reegar for help. But, as it was, she paused and sent a quick notice to Argus.

A moment later, she got a thumbs-up, two hearts, and a black cat.

"Gentlemen, I am yours for the day, but I have an event this evening. I need to be home for that."

Iofer blinked, and she could swear that his ears flapped a little. "Of course. Right, well, this way, then. Time is of the essence."

She nodded and waved toward the door. "After you."

The elf, the goblin, and the troll wearing sunglasses surrounded her and escorted her to their vehicle.

The moment she was inside, she was urged to buckle up, and as the click locked her in, the SUV took off.

"We are going to use a mobile transport, Ms. Mirrin. Please relax and don't fight the magic."

Imara nodded and sat back against the polished seat. Next to her, the troll took some gulping breaths, and she reached out and held his hand while they were surrounded by magic and pulled through space.

The moment they stopped, Henry opened the door and threw up.

She unbuckled and got out. "Now, will someone tell me what I am supposed to do?"

Feel it, Imara. There is one of those stones here... and it isn't good.

She extended her senses and found the stone. "Aww, shit."

The lot where they had stopped was outside a Mage Guild office, and as she ran toward the pull of magic, Iofer, Morgig and a still-green Henry surrounded her to give her a mobile escort.

The underground parking lot was filled with panicked guild officers. The XIA pushed them aside and showed her the problem.

"What do you want me to do with it when I get it out?"

One of the officers asked, "Who are you?"

She scowled at him. "A Death Keeper. Who are you?"

He was elbowed aside, his golden good looks ignored by those around him.

"We need the stone contained by whatever means you can arrange."

She nodded and looked down at the woman who had a dozen dead mages trying to take over her body.

Her right hand was clenched, and the flickers of power were running through her.

"What is her name?"

"Officer Corral."

Imara sighed. "Her first name."

The older officer crouched next to Imara. "Etta. Her name is Etta. She has two brothers, a sister, and is the fourth generation to be an officer. She was cleaning out and bagging evidence from this vehicle, and she touched the stone. The Death Keepers recommended you."

She nodded. "Right. Not many of them would like to do this."

Mr. E, get to safety.

You need me.

You can take the overspill. I don't want you taken over. If these guys are aggressive, I am going to have to drain them. That will be messy.

"If I could get a little more space, please. This will throw off a bit of power."

The crowd shuffled back a few inches, but Imara didn't care. She was where she needed to be with her kitten out of touching range.

"Etta, my name is Imara. I am here to help."

She frantically shook her head, but Imara placed her hand over the hand clutched to Etta's chest. The dynamic of power shifted rapidly, and the heat from the stone localized.

"Let go of it, Etta. Push the spirits out of you and give me the stone. This is what I am trained for. I will be fine."

Etta's eyes resumed a beautiful cornflower blue. "Don't. Don't, it hurts!"

"I know." Imara took Etta's hand and turned it over. She was using all of her concentration to subdue the spectral energy, but she needed to keep Etta calm.

She smiled and said softly, "When she is free, pull her out of the way. I am going to need to bleed off some power."

She glanced around her quickly, and the XIA were ready to take action. It appeared that Etta was on their team.

"Okay, I am taking it in three, two, one..." She eased the stone free of the mage, and the world went white.

Chapter Eight

$\mathcal{T}$he roar of her hellcat brought her back, and she looked down at those gathered. *Fuck.* She was hovering.

You are ours now. You will be our limbs, our eyes, our touch.

Fuck you and your little dead brains. You are going to discover something surprising right about now.

She vented the power through the large feline version of Mr. E. He scrubbed the power and dumped the clean energy back into Etta, who was being held by Iofer a few feet away.

What? What are you doing? We will be free!

You will return to the wave. Con-

gratulations.

Once Etta was returned to stable, Imara topped up the XIA with the spectral energy, and then, she let the rest power off through the open doors of the car park and out into the surrounding flora and fauna.

The scrubbed energy was powerful, but Imara didn't give anyone else a drop of it. She took the last remnant of twelve mages and left only a vague murmur of their energies so she could identify them later.

With a smile, she made a small kissy noise, and Mr. E shrank and hopped back on her shoulder. "Okay, so how am I getting home?"

Iofer held Etta close, and she was sobbing onto his shoulder. "We will take you back, but it is a four-hour drive."

She nodded. "Right."

The older man who appeared to be in charge said, "What just happened here?"

Imara blinked. "Which city am I in?"

"Leobrad Municipality. Where are you from?"

She sighed and rubbed her head with the hand not holding the deadly crystal. "Depford College."

His eyes widened. "How did they find you?"

She wrinkled her nose. "Do you have a vial or some kind of containment for the crystal?"

"No. I don't want that thing in my guild."

She fought the urge to sigh. "Right. Well, can someone get me a coffee, two sugars, two creams? This has been a long fucking night."

The gathered might of the Leobrad guild offices stared at her.

She sighed and used her free hand to scroll through her phone for Adrea's number.

"Ritual space, Adrea speaking."

"Hiya, Adrea. This is Imara."

"Oh, hi! How did your exam go?"

"Pretty good, are you willing to take on another stone? I have one here in my hand, and no one wants to take it on."

"Sure? When?"

"Three hours if I can get a lift." She looked around, and none of the mages would meet her gaze. "Just a moment."

She looked at the guy in charge. "Can someone take me to the transport station, at least?"

A shadow fell across the door to the garage. "We'll take you home." The voice was feminine and amused.

Mr. E bristled. *Demon magic.*

Not truly. Check it again. It is much a demon as you are an actual cat. If they are willing to give me a ride, I will take it.

I...

Hold your objections until we can get home. Then you can give me your as-

sessment.

Yes, Imara.

She could feel him sulking against her neck.

"I will take that ride, please."

She turned to Iofer. "She will be fine. I will send you a report as to the construction of this particular stone by the weekend. I am going to have to pull the spectres apart, and that takes time."

"Thank you, Ms. Mirrin. I am sorry that we can't take you back, but this crew was heading that way anyway, and they answered while you were floating."

"How long was I floating?"

Iofer blinked. "About an hour."

"Dammit. Thanks. Have Etta contact me if there are any side effects beyond trauma. Contact a counsellor for that."

She kept her fist closed over the stone but tried to keep it relaxed. Mr. E was not going to be in the mood to swallow this one for storage.

She walked toward the female shadow and smiled. "Hiya, I am Imara Mirrin, stranded Death Keeper."

The other woman smiled and extended her hand, "I am Benny, blended mage and our Mage Guild's contribution to my XIA team."

Imara felt tremendous power in the woman's hand, and the eyes that she looked into were stamped with fey energy.

When they approached the vehicle, the guys were out and leaning against it. They all had the excellent physical tone that most of the XIA sported, and their gazes on Benny were possessive.

"Oh, this isn't going to be an uncomfortable ride at all," Imara muttered.

Benny chuckled. "I will sit between you and Tremble. Smith is driving, and Argyle will be co-piloting."

"Thanks. My familiar is named Mr. E, and he is a little touchy right now."

Benny chuckled, and she nodded for the guys to get in the vehicle. "Demon hunter?"

"Me? No."

"No, your familiar. He has the look of an inherited familiar, and those tend to be folks who displeased the Mage Guild. His bristling when he identified me is a pretty good sign that he doesn't like mages with demon blood."

The other three settled in the vehicle, Benny slid into the centre of the back seat, and Imara got in, closing the door awkwardly before settling in. Not being able to use her hand was difficult, but letting that power go in this small space with the shifter, the fey, and the vampire wearing shades, was not a great idea.

Buckle up.

"I can't buckle up without my hand."

Benny smiled. "I will give you a hand with that."

A moment later, after the stranger

had leaned over her and tucked her in, they were on their way.

"How did you know about my familiar?"

"One of my best friends is a hellhound. She is locked into her servitude, and she was born into it. I am guessing that he is a generated one, which makes him an ancient mage, which makes him one of the demon hunters. Everybody else just went from spectre to flecks of energy."

"You... you have studied."

The elf, Tremble, leaned over. "Her family is in possession of the largest library of spells and magical lore in the country."

She blinked. "You are Beneficia Ganger?"

Benny beamed. "That's the one. You have done some studying yourself."

"Oh, wow. I read a book by one of your ancestors. It helped me solve a problem."

"Really? Which one?"

"Lenora Ganger."

"Oh, that's my mom. She's older than she looks." Benny smiled. "Was it a textbook?"

"Oh. No. It was a romance and a diary rolled into one."

Smith was the shifter; he looked back at her in the mirror and grinned. "I think Benny might be willing to trade you for that one. It doesn't seem that she has it."

"It isn't mine to trade."

Benny smiled. "To whom does it belong?"

"The owner of Reegar Hall. That is where I live."

Benny's expression was shocked. "I used to visit Reegar Hall. I don't remember who owned it, though."

"Technically, the college owns it, but Reegar is the spectre of the hall. It is his support, and it keeps him going."

Tremble piped up, "He was mourned by one of my clan."

"Liirick?"

Tremble nodded. "How did you know?"

"He comes by, and he and Reegar knock boots now and then. Mostly, when he is doing speaking engagements at the college."

Tremble looked around Benny in astonishment. "How is that possible?"

Imara wrinkled her nose. "I am a Death Keeper. My passive talent is boosting the presence of the spectres. Reegar is as solid as he wants to be."

Argyle turned around in his seat, and he gave her a piercing look with his red gaze. "Are you single?"

"No. I have a boyfriend."

Benny grinned. "Do tell. We have a long drive before we get to the college."

"Oh, can we stop at Ritual Space? I

have to drop this off." She held up her closed fist.

Smith nodded. "Wherever you need to go. Iofer says that you saved their teammate." Smith grinned before he turned back to driving. "And we can go very fast."

The acceleration to the interstate was very tangible.

Benny turned to her again. "So, tell me about your fella or lady, and then, let me know what is clenched in your hand and why is it turning black?"

Imara sighed. "I am holding the spectral amalgamation of seventeen mages who were not pleasant men. There has been a rash of these kinds of stones recently. The right combination of faded spectres can make an incredibly powerful talisman, but this one is just dangerous."

"And why is your hand turning black?"

She grumbled, "It is trying to take power from me, so I have to deaden the area for containment. It will be fine, I hope."

Benny frowned. "Well, while we rocket down the highway, I am going to return to the topic I am interested in. How did you meet your boyfriend?"

Imara wrinkled her nose. "We met in class."

"Aww, did he help you with your homework?" Argyle had a strange sing-song to his voice.

"No, he helped me with a skeevy instructor, and I helped him with his homework." She smirked and checked the stone. There was a little leakage, so she had to change her technique. Argyle was getting influenced.

She pulled in the energy she needed to contain the stone and let the band of black form around her wrist. She watched the vampire shake his head to clear it.

Benny raised her brows. "What was that?"

"Leakage. The technically undead are more susceptible. Sorry, Argyle. I have it now."

Mr. E crept down her arm. *Let me have it. This is doing damage to you.*

Are you okay with the occupants of the vehicle?

Yes. My investigations indicate that their link to the demon king who spawned them has been severed. It is a daring and complicated move. I must say, I am impressed, now give me the stone before it hurts you.

Thank you. If it gives you trouble, I will take it back.

"My familiar is going to take the stone. There is going to be a bit of a release of power, and then, things should be fine." She watched the kitten crouch over the stone, and when he gave her a slight nod, she opened her hand.

A slight flare of energy and the pulse of power shut off. The colour started to return to her hand immediately.

"Thanks, Mr. E." She smiled, and he walked over to her lap and curled up.

"Wow. Is he seriously a kitten?" Benny's fingers were flexing.

"Yes, but wait until he has hacked up the stone before you try and pet him. He has warmed to the demon influence in you and your men, but he isn't a fan in general."

Tremble laughed. "He picked up on that?"

"Your connection? No, your posture on your vehicle did. You were all equal, and all fixated on Benny's walk. That indicated intimacy."

Smith nodded. "Body language is key. What do you and your boyfriend do for private time?"

She smirked. "We find a public place

and go to a movie or something. No sex until I finish college. Mr. E is willing to enforce it."

The entire group was shocked. Imara laughed, and Mr. E started purring. It was interesting. She had never murdered a conversation before.

Chapter Nine

They made the three-hour trip to Ritual Space in ninety minutes. Mr. E was growing cool with his efforts to contain the spectres, and she wanted to get it out of him.

Adrea came out to the parking area with a smile that turned into delight. "Benny!"

Benny passed Tremble and hugged Adrea.

Imara undid her seatbelt and carefully carried Mr. E to the proprietor of Ritual Space. "Hi, Adrea."

Adrea came forward and hugged her as well, her white hair swinging around her face. "Not again. Okay, come this way."

"If Blueberry is in, he can lead me to the stones."

"Of course. I will see you when everything is contained."

Imara nodded and clutched her limp familiar to her as she entered the space. Blueberry was waiting, and he hopped ahead of her at a good pace, leaving her to stride after him and into the space between realities where it was safe to store this sort of spirit.

Blueberry sat next to the open gateway on his hind legs, and his expression indicated that he was willing to wait.

Imara set Mr. E down on the wide stone bench, and she tickled him. He kicked his legs and opened his eyes.

"Hack it up."

She petted his fur and held him as he started hacking. For a moment, it seemed that it wouldn't come up, but then, the small crystal dropped to the stone.

She sighed and picked up Mr. E with one hand while placing the stone into the arc above the bench.

"Right. Gentlemen, I want the bossiest of you to come out now." She sent a trickle of power into the stone, and a torso formed above the containment band.

"I don't need to talk to a lowly mage."

"I am not just a mage, but keep insulting me. I will just do this."

She grabbed his energy and tore it apart, shredding it into particles so small that they were only good for blending with the next wave.

Sighing, she spoke to the stone. "I will return, I will question all of you, and I want to know who you are. If you give me a satisfactory answer, I will put you into a soul stone and give you a second life as a rejuvenated spectre. Think it over."

She turned and cuddled her kitten while following the bunny down the trail that only existed when she was moving to that pocket between worlds.

Blueberry led her to the rear patio where the garden was flourishing, and some small tables had been assembled so that Adrea could serve tea. The XIA team was sitting around and eating scones.

"Imara, are you done?"

She nodded. "For today. I will still have to come back to conduct interviews."

"Aside from the one you dispersed."

"Yeah, that. He was just an asshole."

Benny blinked. "You destroyed a spectre?"

"Sure. It's not tricky." Imara sat in the empty seat that was waiting for her.

Adrea patted her on the shoulder. "Don't be smug."

Imara blinked. "It isn't being smug.

Anyone with magical skills can tear apart a spectre. Being a Death Keeper just means I can tear it up really, really small."

Benny laughed. "Fair enough. So, you have been here before?"

Adrea snorted. "Every two days for the last six weeks. Hyl has been tutoring her for her class."

Smith looked at her in genuine surprise. "*Hyl* has been tutoring you?"

"Yes." She petted Mr. E with one hand while sipping her tea with the other.

Argyle was sitting in the shade, but he asked, "What is your class?"

"Stealth Magic. He taught me how to move and a few spells to assist in my final project, which—thankfully—was completed."

Tremble arched his pale brows. "Did you pass?"

"I completed the exam. That is a

pass."

She checked her phone and smiled at the text from Argus.

Etta is doing well, Iofer is worshiping the very idea of you, and his team has pledged allegiance to you. Are you home?

She texted back. *Ritual Space. Had to drop off the annoying item.*

Benny smiled. "The boyfriend. I can tell by your expression."

"Yeah. He was just checking in."

Adrea rolled her eyes. "He checks in a lot. I swear, I was almost hoping for a crime spree just to stop her phone from going off."

The XIA officers looked at each other in surprise.

Smith asked, "Crime spree?"

Adrea grinned. "Didn't she tell you? She is dating Argus. He has been hanging around here with annoying frequency while she was training, though he did bring excellent ice cream every time, so that says something."

Imara started to blush. "I like sugar after a lot of magic expenditure."

Smith was still staring. "Argus? *Our* Argus?"

Imara grinned. "Technically, I have dibs on him, but that particular claiming is still six months or so away. I have to get my accreditation from the Mage Guild to be a commercial mage, but I inherited a building from a friend of mine, so my offices are set. No romantic entanglements until I have my professional life in place."

Benny stared. "How old are you?"

"Twenty. I will still be twenty by the time I graduate."

"How did you and Argus meet?"

Imara chuckled. "I told you. I met him in class. Ethics class. He had to take a course for work, and he helped me out with my shape shifting course."

Benny was enthralled. "You can shape shift?"

"Yeah. I passed the class."

Smith challenged, "What is your beast?"

"You are going to laugh."

Smith held up a hand. "I promise to try not to."

"Griffin vulture."

Mr. E perked up at the cacophony of laughter that surrounded them. *What is going on?*

I said something funny. Are you okay?

He was very strong.

He is a celestial smear now.

Good. When can we go home?

I am hoping that we will be on our way shortly.

Adrea settled and smiled. "This quartet had their bonding ceremony here. It was just after I had taken over and a nice way to start my life in this place. You might want to consider it when you and Argus want to tie the knot."

"There is no proposal in the air."

Adrea snorted. "I would have to be blind to miss the bonding with you two; now, eat two scones with cream and jam, and I will let you go. Until then, no one is going to make a move for the door."

Imara looked, and the other four were frozen in time. "I hate it when you do that."

"There is no other way for you to gain the skills you did. You got six months' worth of training in six weeks. I had to slow time here to achieve it. And it was fun. Mostly fun." Adrea winked and waved at her to load up the scones. "I wasn't kidding. Two scones with cream and jam. Go. And then, I will let them loose."

Imara put some clotted cream on a plate for Mr. E and set up her two scones. One was blackberry and one strawberry, both had cream.

She chewed her way through them with deliberation, and when the final bite was in her mouth, the other four were released from time.

Mr. E was sitting on the table and enjoying his cream, and the others looked a little disconcerted at her jam-stained face.

Benny blinked. "Did we miss something?"

"Nope. Just Adrea throwing her weight around."

Adrea crossed her arms. "Imara doesn't eat properly, and she burns a lot of energy. She's the seventh child of a seventh child twice over. She's got so much luck, it is dizzying."

"Love you, too, Addy." After wiping her lips, she blew Adrea a kiss.

"I can give you a ride home, Imara." Argus's voice was behind her.

She turned her head, and he set his hand on her shoulder. "That would be great. Mr. E isn't really comfortable."

Argus looked over her shoulder at her familiar. "Aw, he looks exhausted."

Smith cleared his throat. "Argus, when were you going to mention your lady friend here?"

Argus squeezed her shoulder. "When it was any of your business, Smith. Argyle, Tremble, Benny, nice to see you all."

Smith winced. "Right. Got it. Imara is an incredible choice. She deserves better than you."

"Yes, I am aware, but she keeps saying that she got lucky."

"I did. Well, this has been fun, but I have to grab my kitten and go. We both need a bit of rest before I get to meet my family tonight."

That got everyone except Adrea curious.

Imara held up her hand. "Too long to explain. If we ever meet again, I am sure I will be happy to fill you in."

She got up and cuddled a sleepy Mr. E against her chest. "Lovely to meet you. Have to run. Have a great day, and thanks for the ride."

Argus put his arm around her, and he supported her very tired self out to his vehicle.

"So, everybody else is off shift?"

"Yeah, lucky for you I don't need much sleep. You look haggard but love-ly."

She laughed softly and buckled in with Mr. E on her lap. She poured a bit of energy into him, and he sat up, stretching.

"Thanks, Argus. I want nothing more than my own bed. I have to brace for my family party this evening."

"Do you need me there?"

"No, but be braced for a call if the

Mage Guild can't manage it. I am pretty sure that there is going to be a riot by midnight."

She slumped over and leaned against his shoulder.

"You sound like you have had a long day. What happened with Iofer?"

"They came by the house and asked for my help. They used an emergency transport spell that spit us out in their home city. I am guessing that it was their mage component that had touched the stone, the stone started using living energy to propel the spirits, and she went down. I don't know how long she had been there, but those mages were useless.

"Anyway, I get there, I take possession of the stone, get it contained, bleed off the extra energy and give it back to the XIA team members. From there, I was looking for a ride home. The XIA agents couldn't manage it with their wounded member, the Mage Guild didn't want to come near me because I had arrived with the extranaturals. Benny and her team came in just at the right time."

"They are a solid unit. I don't know what their assignment was, but I am glad that they were there."

"As am I. I will get you home in one piece. Just rest. I will wake you when Bara is glaring at me out of the window."

"Thanks, Argus. It has been a hectic few hours."

"I gathered as much, but when Iofer sent out the call for help, I knew you could manage the job. Glad you made it, now sleep."

She breathed in, breathed out, and the world went warmly dark.

Low voices surrounded her, and she was carried and settled down on the couch in the common room. She opened her eyes just enough to see Reegar, Bara, and Argus, and she could feel Mr. E.

"Wake me at six, so I can get ready for the party."

Reegar frowned. "You need a healer."

"That can wait until tomorrow. Today, I just need some rest."

Argus sat next to her, holding her hand, and the other two disappeared.

She opened her eyes a little wider and sighed. "Thanks for getting me home."

"No problem. I am happy to have been there." He stroked her cheek.

"I still have to write that report on the spectres. Someone seems to be looking for something, and they aren't waiting for the dissipated ones anymore. They are grabbing some really strong spectres and smashing them together. That isn't good."

"I know. I have learned that much from you."

She sniffed. "Do I smell food?"

"It has been decided that you will get more of a boost from a large infusion of food than simple rest."

She groaned. "Everybody is trying to feed me today."

"Adrea?"

"Yeah, and she paused time to do it. That is one scary lady when she wants you to eat a scone."

He chuckled and gave her a light kiss. "There are a bunch of scary ladies out there; you just have to find their triggers. Apparently, Adrea's is knowing that you need food after magic."

"Why do folks fuss over me?"

Reegar came into her field of view with a tray in his hands. "Because you are young, and you are fearless. It makes us worry."

Argus nodded and helped her sit up.

"Oh, this isn't for her. Mr. E looks a little weak, so we defrosted a pie. Imara's food is still on the stove."

Mr. E perked up and looked around. Reegar reached between them and scooped up the fluffy familiar, setting him on the tray, on the coffee table, next to the pie. It didn't take long before the familiar and the pie became one.

Imara talked quietly with Argus and Bara while the kitten romped in the dessert; when her food arrived, it did wonders for her sense of reality and connectivity to the universe.

Bara finally asked, "How did the fabric work? I got it out of your room."

Imara raised her thumb. "It was excellent. It should give you the grade you were looking for as well."

Argus asked, "What fabric?"

Bara smiled. "It was a speciality wrap that could be worn while shifting. I am trying to find a way to make it in something larger than a five-inch strip."

"Can't you stitch it together?"

Bara sighed. "No. That is the problem."

Imara smiled and felt the ripple of relief that she didn't have to tell Argus what she was actually using it for. He was in law enforcement, and until she was officially invited into the home of Desmond Demiel, she had committed a crime.

No pressure.

Chapter Ten

Formal clothing was easy when you had someone still majoring in textiles under your roof. The gown that Bara had prepared for her took her breath away. Long, silky panels of black and blue wrapped in a five-inch wide belt studded with jet beads. The gown made her feel very adult, and it matched with her black Death Keeper robes.

The invitation to her father's birthday and her niece's family blessing had mentioned wearing honours. She was wearing her honours. The embroidery that Kitigan's family had created was stunning. All she needed was a staff, and she would be at home in any formal death-related setting.

Imara tucked her phone into the pocket in her belt and looked at Mr. E. "How do I look?"

Excellent. I will be on guard this evening. You know they are going to try and trip you up.

She nodded. "I know. At least I have confirmation from my instructor that I passed with ninety-percent in the stealth magic course. Phone, email and the photo. It was nice of Argus to make him make those calls."

You have the photo?

"On my phone and two copies printed. Bara has one copy and Reegar the other. Both are locked up and in a stasis field."

Do you feel paranoid?

She nodded. "Yes, but I am going to see family. From my research, that is an appropriate feeling."

He snickered and jumped to the

shoulder of her robes. She had her invitation, the gift for the baby, she had her familiar, and she had her formalwear. She was ready to face the part of her family that had thrown her away.

A deep exhalation and she walked down to Kitigan's car. She was her designated driver for the evening, and her vehicle was new and a nice SUV.

"So, Imara, when you want to leave, call me. If anything goes weird, call me. If Mr. E hacks up a hairball, call me."

Mr. E lifted his head and made a cute noise.

"I promise. If I don't get furious and fly home, I will definitely call you."

"Good. Now, get in the car." Kitty held the door open and made sure that the robes and the dress were safe and tidy.

The rest of the drive was basically silent with the exception of Imara making one call.

"Are you ready?"

The voice on the other end said, "I don't sleep."

She ended the call and tucked her phone back into her belt. "Whoo."

"It will be fine. Everyone will be fine."

Imara glanced over. "My family is going to hate me."

Kitty chuckled. "They already hate you."

"This is true. Thanks for that." Imara grinned, and she relaxed and petted Mr. E the entire way to Demiel Hall.

"Call me when you want to leave. I will just be around the corner at that donut shop. I brought some homework with me, so don't rush it." Kitty grinned as she pulled into the circular drive in front of the wide and ancient hall.

"Will do. Happy studying." She opened her door and slid onto the crunchy black gravel.

Mr. E popped up and perched proudly on her shoulder. *I am going to be on alert tonight.*

Thanks. Me too.

With her back braced and her robes hanging straight, she walked up to the double doors, and they were swung open by two trolls in uniform.

She smiled and inclined her head. "Good evening. I am here for the party."

One of the trolls extended his hand, and she produced the invitation. He peered down and inclined his head. "Go through to the ballroom."

She patted his hand and smiled. "Thank you. I think that is the most polite thing I will hear this evening."

He looked surprised, and he gave her a slow, toothy smile. "Welcome, Death Keeper."

She nodded and remembered that that is what she was here. She was a powerful mage invited to an event. That was all.

The huge archway in front of her was glowing with light. She tucked her invitation into her belt and walked through the security spell.

A human butler stood by and held out his hand for the invitation. She pulled it smoothly from her belt and handed it to him.

He frowned, looked at her robes, and then announced her to the room of strange but rather familiar faces in the room. "Master Death Keeper, Imara Mirrin Deepford-Smythe."

Technically, it was her name, though Imara Mirrin was acceptable for legal purposes.

The man who had to be her father strode forward. He glared down at her but didn't speak.

A young woman came to his side and clung to him. "Didn't they take your coat at the door?"

Imara raised her brows. "This is my

formal garb, just as every man here is wearing his own master's robes."

She blinked and frowned. "They don't look the same."

"They would not be. I am not a master mage."

That seemed to satisfy her. "That's it. What do you do?"

Imara inclined her head. "This and that."

"What are you doing, calling yourself a Death Keeper? Their branch of the guild is exceptionally strict. Wearing those robes could get you bound by law." Desmond was trying to intimidate her.

"I am aware of that. It is why I proudly wear the rank earned by hundreds of hours of work with spectres. There are four in this building alone, are there not?"

He blinked. "You can't be serious."

"I can. If you are my father, happy birthday, by the way."

The young woman jolted. She might be four or five years older than Imara, but her attitude was much younger.

He extended his hand in greeting, and she knew it was to test her power.

She extended her hand, and their grip generated blue and crimson lightning throughout the room.

He released her and smiled. "It is a pleasure to finally meet you, daughter."

"And you as well, Master Demiel. Now, may I bring out the spectres and have them join the party?"

He shrugged, and the doubt was still in him. "As you like. Your brothers are here and will introduce themselves and their wives. You are welcome at Demiel Hall."

She nodded. "Thank you for your welcome; now, let the deceased join us."

She powered up the spectres to the point where they appeared solid, and they began to migrate toward the party.

Luken smiled at her and came over. "Come on, let me introduce you."

She leaned toward him. "I hope it gets less tense."

"Probably won't. Let's start with the baby. She's friendly."

Imara laughed and walked with her twin to meet her oldest brother, his wife, and their new baby.

The baby was genuinely a newborn. "She's adorable."

Her brother, Michael, and his wife, Hannah, watched her for a moment, and then, Hannah seemed to act on impulse and handed the baby over.

Imara blinked and cradled the little one with the pink cheeks and rich blue eyes of a new baby. "Well, I am not technically your aunt due to fun family stuff, but every baby deserves a present."

Imara cradled the baby with one arm and reached into the belt with the other hand, sticking her fingers into the pocket specially made for this purpose. With a light touch, she brushed a tiny smudge across the forehead and then the back of each tiny fist. "Congratulations on the magic, little one."

Hannah smiled and whispered, "Imara."

"What?"

"Her name is Imara Rose. We call her Rosie for short, but Michael felt this was right."

Imara grinned as the smudges disappeared and the baby's bright blue eyes got a little brighter. "In that case, this is a very good gift."

Hannah asked, "What was that stuff?"

Imara chuckled. "Dirt from the site of the last local wave of magic. It will give her a grounding when it comes to learning and the ability to call on nature for what she needs. Perhaps we can get another family member through the sky breaking course."

Luken groaned. "Don't tell me you got in."

"I did. It was a fun course but hard as hell. You were never doing what you thought you were until you suddenly got it right."

One of her nearest brothers walked over. "How did you get in?"

Luken made the introductions. "Edmund, this is Imara, Imara, Edmund. His twin is Edgar."

Imara reached out for Edmund's hand, but he didn't take it.

"How did you get in?"

"I passed the aptitude test. It was as simple as that. If you didn't get in, then the course would have killed you."

Michael was frowning. "Edmund, why are you being rude?"

He hissed. "She doesn't belong here. She's stringing everybody along, making them think she is a true mage, a true talent, but we all know she was eighth. She is unlucky."

Luken looked at Edmund. "Are you nuts? You know the truth."

"Dad says it's a lie. She was eighth. There was no doubt in his mind."

Imara pinched the bridge of her nose. "Right. And he wasn't in the room for any of the deliveries. Oh, and on my birth certificate, it lists my birth as a minute earlier. Oh, and our mother says I was seventh. For someone supposed to be unlucky, I do tend to be in the right place at the right time to help those around me. If you want to argue that, feel free, but you had better bring back-up."

Edmund flushed and spun around, stalking over to their father.

She looked to Luken. "Is there anyone else I can alienate while I am here?"

She handed the baby back to her mother after stroking her cheek one more time. "Bye, Rosie."

Her married brothers were all fairly calm; it was the three in school that were tense. Michael, Alexander, and Desmond Jr. were all fine. They had achieved their Master status and were relaxed. Edmund, Richard and supposedly Edgar were all tense. Luken wasn't, but he was lucky. That explained that.

The spectres came to her, and they all smiled and spoke favourably. Lord Demiel, Lady Demiel, and their two children, Halos and Nyxos, had been spectres since a plague had swept them away over a hundred and fifty years earlier.

Desmond came over. "Who are these folk? How did they get in?"

Imara blinked. "They are the spectres of Demiel Hall. They have been here the entire time."

He paused, and Edmund shifted eagerly behind him.

Lord Demiel stood between them.

Imara glanced over her shoulder and nearly choked. The portrait of Lord Demiel was right behind him.

"Tell me something that only my ancestor would know."

Lord Demiel looked offended, but he leaned forward and whispered in Desmond's ear. Whatever he said made Desmond stand upright immediately.

"I... I thought you spectres too weak to speak."

"We were. This Death Keeper of Demiel blood offered us her energy, and now, we can interact with the world again. Well, we can interact with the world within these walls. She is exceptionally powerful. You should be proud as it is your blood in her veins. She is clever."

Desmond turned to Imara. "You may leave now."

She nodded and turned to the spectres. "I offer you a physical presence for a month or two."

Lady Demiel smiled. "We will take it."

"The house is yours." Imara smiled at the few friendly siblings she had, and she left the same way she had come while the spectres exclaimed at their physical presence. That was going to mess with her father and his bride for a while.

The power sparked as she left, and she grinned. The building was being warded against her. They needed her physical presence to drop a barrier against her. She had had to be invited in, so she could be locked out.

She patted each of the trolls on the hand as she left, and Mr. E started to purr the instant her feet stepped on the walkway.

She fished out her phone and dialled Kitty. "Hello, Kitty. I am done here."

"Great. I will be there in a minute."

"I am walking toward the donut shop,

so don't rush. I think I need time to clear my head."

"Excellent. I am still getting into my car." Kitty chuckled.

"See ya soon."

The call ended, and Imara kept walking until she was off the grounds and onto the road.

You handled that well.

She chuckled. "We know why I was invited, so it is nice to have that confirmation. They think they have what they need, so they booted me out. It rings a bell."

You didn't remember the first time.

"Ah, you know that I got to read it out in black and white. Mom wasn't even allowed to keep me because of that contract."

And that was in the past, and you are now an adult with a cooler head for your situation. You still have luck, friends, and a mom who is just getting to know you.

She grinned and kept walking. "I know. I am not bitter. I am feeling better now that I am away from them. That is one toxic atmosphere. At least Michael and Hannah seem pretty normal, and Rosie is a cutie."

She is very cute. If you see her when she is older, I sense tail pulling in my future.

Imara giggled until Kitty pulled up next to her and rolled down the window. "Hey, little lady, going my way?"

"Kitty, I am going to give you such a butt kicking." She walked around and got in on the passenger side.

When she was buckled up and Mr. E was on the dashboard, she sat back and sighed. "Home, Jeeves."

"Yes, madam." Kitty put the vehicle in drive, and the trip home began.

Imara could hardly wait to see what had happened at Reegar Hall while she had been gone.

Chapter Eleven

Imara got out of the car with a groan, and Mr. E perched on her shoulder. Kitty grabbed her books and headed off to finish her homework elsewhere.

When Imara came through the doors, she paused and blinked. "Wow, this is a little more active than I thought it would be."

Edgar Demiel was tied up on the floor and gagged. Bara was baking cookies, and Reegar was going through a pile of books that had been spilled to the floor.

The security officers were taking a statement from Bara while she baked to calm down.

Imara checked her watch, and she

nodded. A quick photo and an email later and she introduced herself to the security officers.

Reegar growled, "Get him out of here."

Imara nodded. "Good evening, officers. I see there has been an intrusion."

Bara sniffled. "It was horrible, Imara. I heard a noise upstairs, and that guy was there, tangled in my loom. He ruined three weeks of weaving! I am never going to get my ninety-five percent in that class now."

Imara kept her face concerned. Bara's drama courses were paying off.

The security officers kept making notes. One asked, "Who are you, miss?"

"I am Imara Mirrin."

"Do you know who this man is?"

She looked at Edgar and bit her lip. "I think he is in one of my classes. I haven't been formally introduced, but I am pretty sure we are related."

The officers looked confused by that. "What is his name?"

"His last name is Demiel."

Both officers lowered their notepads. She gave them a bland look. "And I am Imara Mirrin Deepford-Smythe Demiel. He broke into my house, and I don't know what he wanted. I will assist Mage Reegar with pressing charges for any broken materials, and compensation should be issued to Bara for the destruction of her weaving project. It does look good on him, doesn't it?"

Edgar was flushed and furious, writhing from side to side.

The notebooks came back up. "What did he try and take?"

Reegar scowled. "He was rifling through my books."

One of the officers thought to ask, "What class were you in with him?"

"Stealth Magic. Don't worry; his deadline was forty-five minutes ago."

She smiled and inclined her head.

The officers had tensed, and then, they smiled at each other with a smug air.

Imara knew that Edgar was going to fail the course, but she also knew he would get off without any consequences. Her checks on Demiel history showed that they were primarily bullies who liked to throw money around.

Just as they were hauling Edgar to his feet, with the gag still in place, the door opened, and Hyl arrived. He smiled at Imara and paused to stare at her brother. "What is this?"

Bara sobbed and set the cookie batter down with a thud. "HebrokeinandwreckedmyprojectandtoreitupandthrewbooksaroundandnowtheyaregoingtolethimgobecauseheisaDemiel."

Hyl grabbed Edgar by the shoulder, his Mage Guild uniform neat and tidy, and his eyes twinkling. "Did he use magic to break in?"

Reegar nodded. "He did. He used a spell to break through the glass, but he still managed to do a lot of manual damage."

"Using magic during the commission of a crime is a serious offense."

He pulled the gag from Edgar's mouth. "Did you use magic in the commission of a crime?"

"It was my assignment. I had to!" Edgar was nearly foaming with fury. "She has a stone stolen from my house! Check her!"

Mr. E jumped down, so Imara could remove her robes and hand them to Hyl. There was no way that anything could have been hidden in her gown. She undid her belt and handed it to him.

He checked everything, handed it to the security officers to check, and he looked to Edgar. "So, that is one lie."

"It was her assignment! She had to! Ask her! She was at Demiel Hall tonight. She had to have stolen it, or she is going to fail."

Hyl raised his brows at Imara. "Were you at the hall tonight?"

"I was. I was surrounded at all times and left promptly at midnight when requested. It was a little cold blooded of them actually."

He nodded. "You have completed your courses?"

"I have. I have emails, a voicemail, and a photo indicating that my course is complete and was complete before this evening."

Hyl grinned. "Excellent. Well, I will take this young mage and have him up on charges of magic outside of scholastic purpose."

Edgar's eyes were wild. "It was an assignment."

Hyl looked at him blandly. "It was

stealth magic. What sounds stealthy to you about your actions this evening?"

Imara watched as her tutor left her hall with the officers trying to figure out how to get on the guild's good side.

Bara started to scoop out the cookies, and she grinned over at Imara. "How was your family?"

"Half nice, half horrible. What kind of cookies?"

"Chocolate and peanut butter. I kept some of the dough without chocolate for Mr. E. He looks like he has been hard at work keeping you calm."

Mr. E jumped on the table and perched up like a prairie dog. Bara made tiny balls of dough for him and set it out on a plate.

Reegar sighed. "You were right; he is after the demon codex."

Mr. E paused and looked over at Reegar.

Imara moved forward and petted her

familiar. "It is a book belonging to Reegar. Part of his collection, but I am fairly sure that Edgar would not bring it back after stealing it. That book in the hands of the Demiels is a nightmare."

He calmed and continued consuming his treat.

A call brought Kitty over for a post-mortem of the evening and some cookies.

They all sat around the table while Reegar continued to work on the dents and dings his books had taken.

Kitty munched a cookie and smiled. "So. What is your general impression of your family?"

"They are half good, half bad, and not to be trusted. I think I will stick with my mom's side. Her folk are broke, but they have character." She looked at Bara. "I mean, aside from Luken. He's great."

Bara raised her cup of hot cocoa in a

toast. "To Luken!"

Kitty and Imara followed suit. "To Luken."

They all sipped hot cocoa and sat back at two in the morning.

"When do you go to your final class?"

"Tomorrow morning."

Bara frowned. "You need to get some rest. You have had a stressful couple of days."

"Yes, ma'am. See you in the morning."

Mr. E ran ahead of her, up the stairs and into her room. Her wards were still in place against members of her own bloodline, and she dropped to her bed, trying to ignore all of the insults she had absorbed that night.

Don't worry. You are still beloved by your family. Your true family and that gathering is expanding daily.

Thanks, little dude. Sorry you are saddled with me when I am all weepy.

I have had worse mages to deal with. I am truly enjoying myself for the first time in centuries. Keep doing what you are doing and get some sleep.

Imara did as she was told.

The tiny class was a sullen and sombre place. Professor McClairie looked them over. "I told you when this term began that stealth magic is a difficult skill to learn. It is nearly impossible to get the skills together in one short term. Out of the ten of you, only one student managed to exhibit the skills and technique necessary for a passing grade."

Imara was shocked.

"This is not an unusual occurrence, but it was surprising that the student I thought least likely to succeed found the most success. And the object that was drawn was removed, presented and then returned. Unlike most of you, this student took the day of the event literally. The assignment was completed before dawn."

Her classmates were looking like they had been struck with hammers. One asked, "You can do that?"

The professor nodded. "The day begins one minute after midnight."

The professor had folders in his hand, and he went through the students and handed them out. Imara read her name, opened the folder, and her shoulders slumped in relief at the passing grade. Over ninety percent was nothing to sneer at.

Edgar was sitting at the far end of the room, and he got to his feet, stalking toward her. Mr. E hopped off her shoulder and landed on the folder.

He was nearly in front of her when the professor stepped in front of him. "You didn't manage it, Edgar. Get over it. Enroll again next term, and if you display any emotional development, I will consider it. Right now, you are a pathetic rich brat."

Edgar snarled and pulled his fist back. Imara blinked, she hadn't thought that he was the bully in the family, but it seemed that the twins were both assholes.

The professor caught the fist, and he clenched his fingers. Edgar grunted and then began to whine as he was forced to his knees.

"I didn't care for Desmond when he tried and failed this course, and I don't care for you. I know you only took this course to attack your sister here, but it is a shortsighted plan. Get your own path in life. Following orders puts you in unpleasant situations and deprives you of self-sufficiency."

Imara gathered her things and tried to leave, but they were blocking her exit.

Edgar looked over at her with anger

in his expression. "She ruined every-thing."

Imara piped up, "If you are referring to your mother, *our* mother, she was go-ing to leave the moment that she ful-filled the contract. Desmond is an ass."

"You grew up with her!"

She rolled her eyes. "Not this again. I grew up in a group home. I just met my mother, *our* mother, after I arrived here at college. The contract didn't let her keep me. Read it if you don't believe it. No issue of the Demiel line was to re-main in her custody. So, she stuck me in a series of orphanages and homes run by her extended family. I grew up knowing that I was alone and that I was not al-lowed to be with my family. I tried to go and meet you all on your terms, and you tried to break into my fucking home while I was with your twin. He doesn't know how you cock your head when you are getting mad, by the way. He can't fake being you."

He scowled. "I don't believe you."

"Ask her. She will take a call from you. Read the contract. It is available online at the mage contract archive."

Edgar blinked, and she saw the abandoned toddler in his expression. He would have been two when Mirrin left.

"Or don't. Just don't consider me a threat. I won't consider you at all." She climbed on a desk and slithered behind her brother and the professor. She was out the door with her familiar and on her way home in seconds.

She slapped the folder on the table, and Reegar came by to take a look. "Excellent. That is one of the highest scores I have seen."

"You have seen others?"

"Of course. Stealth magic is a hard skill to learn, but a few have an actual knack for it. The hardest part is the professor keeping track of all the temporal trackers that he has out. McClairie is a master at temporal magic."

"Wait, there was a tracker on me?"

"Yes, it is in the notecard he gave that outlined your assignment. It tracked your every move, marked the acquisition of the artifact and, also, marked its return."

She stared at him. "You knew?"

"Yes. I thought it would make you nervous to know about it. It doesn't matter anyway. It is a standard tracking spell."

Imara sighed and looked at her marks, the credits and knew that there was only one class that would give her the credits she needed to finish quickly.

"What are you thinking?"

"My next course. There is only one thing it can be, but it is going to be really dangerous."

I can handle it. I mastered welding

after all.

She wrinkled her nose at him. "Spell Crafting 501. I have managed soul casting, shape shifting, sky breaking and now stealth magic, along with business and ethics courses. So, if I can get spell crafting under my belt, I will be able to get a broad-spectrum magic license. I will have way more skills than I need, but I will qualify for an immediate license. It is that, or they have to kill me."

Reegar grinned. "You have a fascinating career path in mind."

"Yeah. I know. But it just feels right. When it feels right, it feels right."

"What will you do for staff?"

She grinned. "I think that I will pick people with skills I can use, but any of my friends are welcome for work experience when they graduate."

Imara sat back and looked at Reegar. There was no one better to ask. "So, what do I need to know about writing spells?”

Reegar beckoned, and a stack of books began to pile up on the table. More and more came in a huge cascade. “Start here.”

She blinked. “Do I have to lift them? I can do that now.”

He laughed, and she smiled as she prepared to take on the skills that would set her free to live her own life for the first time.

Don't be scared of the future. I will be with you every step of the way.

Imara laughed. “Riding on my shoulder and eating my snacks.”

That is what a familiar is for.

Grinning, she pulled the first tome in front of her and started to read while her other hand finished the registration for the next term. It took three hours for the confirmation to come back, but her path was set. She was going to learn how to craft a spell.

It had better be a good one.

And so ends the fourth book of the Hellkitten Chronicles. Only one left to go.

After book five, *Spell Crafting 501,* the Hellkitten Chronicles will be over, but Imara and Mr. E will become secondary characters with a lot of backstory in *Hellhound in a Handbag,* as well as *Perpetual Prey*. I am working on Imara to get her own HellCat Chronicle, where all of her weird skills can come out and play.

Thanks for reading,

Viola Grace

About the Author

Viola Grace (aka Zenina Masters) is a Canadian sci-fi/paranormal romance writer with ambitions to keep writing for the rest of her life. She specializes in short stories because the thrill of discovery, of all those firsts, is what keeps her writing.

An artist who enjoys a story that catches you up, whirls you around and sets you down with a smile on your face is all she endeavours to be. She prefers to leave the drama to those who are better suited to it, she always goes for the cheap laugh.

www.ingramcontent.com/pod-product-compliance
Lightning Source LLC
Chambersburg PA
CBHW061307210726
48293CB00003B/1156